PRAISE FOR JAMES SCOTT BELL

"Mike Romeo is a terrific hero. He's smart, tough as nails, and fun to hang out with. James Scott Bell is at the top of his game here. There'll be no sleeping till after the story is over." — **John Gilstrap**, New York Times bestselling author of the Jonathan Grave thriller series

"Mike Romeo is a killer thriller hero. And James Scott Bell is a master of the genre." — **Tosca Lee**, New York Times bestselling author

"Mike Romeo is a terrific hard-boiled hero: cage fighter, philosopher, acerbic champion of the underdog. James Scott Bell's series is as sharp as a switchblade." — **Meg Gardiner**, Edgar Award winning author

"Among the top writers in the crowded suspense genre." — **Sheldon Siegel**, New York Times bestselling author

ROMEO'S FIGHT

A Mike Romeo Thriller

JAMES SCOTT BELL

Compendium Press

The best revenge is not to be like your enemy.
— Marcus Aurelius

You can't catch me, I'm the Gingerbread Man.
— "The Gingerbread Man" (children's tale)

ROMEO'S FIGHT

"SO YOU'RE MIKE ROMEO," THE GUY SAID. "YOU DON'T LOOK so tough."

I was sitting poolside at the home of Mr. Zane Donahue, drinking a Corona, and wearing a Hawaiian shirt, shorts, flip-flops and sunglasses. I was the perfect embodiment of L.A. mellow, trying to enjoy a pleasant afternoon. Now this shirtless, tatted-up billboard was planted in front of me, clenching and unclenching his fists.

"I'm really quite personable once you get to know me," I said.

"I don't think you're tough," he said.

"I can recite Emily Dickinson," I said. "Can you?"

He squinted. Or maybe that's how his eyes were naturally. His reddish hair was frizzy. With a little care and coloring, it would have made a nice clown 'do. He had a flat nose, one that had been beaten on pretty good somewhere. In a boxing ring, the cage, or prison.

"Who?" he said.

"You don't know Emily Dickinson?"

Blank stare.

"Then you're not so tough yourself," I said.

I took a sip of my brew and focused on the devil tat above his left nipple. Underneath were the words DIE SCUM. He was one of Donahue's fighters for sure.

There were others of them around the pool, ripped and showing it. And of course the bikini-clad ladies who liked hanging on arms while displaying their own wares. There was a lot of giggling going on. A meeting of the American Philosophical Society this was not.

Zane Donahue himself was behind the swim-up bar, dispensing piña coladas under a Polynesian-themed gazebo.

A DJ bumped dance music from a setup near a large fern by the house. There were maybe fifty people at this thing, and room enough to fit fifty more.

It was a party I did not want to attend, but I owed Donahue a favor. A big one, as he'd given me some invaluable information that helped save a woman's life. And he was not shy about telling me he'd call this favor in.

So here I was, hoping the day could be redeemed with a beer and maybe a swim as I waited to meet with Donahue. But now this knuckle bucket had come over and for some reason wanted to start something.

"You think you can fight?" Mr. Die Scum said. "Bring it."

"What's with the motif?" I said.

"The what?"

"Motif."

"The hell you talkin' about?"

"Hell is exactly right," I said. "As represented by Lucifer there." I pointed. He looked down at his chest, back at me.

Then he kicked the bottom of my right flip-flop.

"Get up," he said.

"I'm comfortable here," I said.

"Get up!"

"And ruin a nice day?"

"Girl," he said.

"Excuse me?"

"Little girl."

"If anything, I'm a big girl," I said.

He kicked my other foot. The heel. My flip-flop flipped off.

I sighed. And put my Corona on the cement deck.

As I stood, Die Scum took a fight stance. People were watching all this. No one moved to stop it.

Some party.

I put my hands up. "If we fight, it's going to be by Dickinson rules."

He frowned. The scar tissue above his right eyebrow gathered into a mini-fist. He was around thirty and starting the fighter's downward slide. Probably in denial about Father Time being undefeated.

"What're you talkin'?" he said.

"Here's what we do," I said. "We give each other a first line from Emily Dickinson, and the other guy has to give the next."

"What?"

"*My river runs to thee.*"

"What the—"

"Wrong," I said. "It's *Blue sea, wilt welcome me.* You lose."

Die Scum's cheeks took on the color of cotton candy.

More of the partiers were shuffling our way. There's always one thing you can tell when you're at a gathering of MMA fighters — when one bull threatens to get it on with another bull, the whole herd closes in to watch.

"Yeah, I heard that about you," Die Scum said. "Big brainiac, likes to show it off."

"That's where you're wrong," I said. "I'd rather people like you understand me. That's why I talk ... so ... slow."

I thrust out with both hands. My right hit the Die Scum tat. My left shoved a skull on the other side of his chest.

Die Scum stumbled backward and fell into the pool.

.   .   .

S ome in the crowd laughed. Some went *Oooh*. A few applauded. Die Scum burst to the surface, shaking his curly head and spraying water like a wet dog, shouting words of fury, scorn, and body parts.

I took off my sunglasses.

Die Scum climbed out of the pool. His face was a blotch-fest of red.

He started for me.

And then Zane Donahue appeared like a bolt of Zeus's lightning. Indeed, the sun lit up the white bathrobe he wore.

"Cool off, guys." Donahue was between us, hands up. "Let's settle this like civilized human beings."

Zane Donahue was rich, fifty or so, fit and connected. Not all the connections were entirely legal.

Die Scum said he wished to remove my head and place it—I believe *shove* is the word he used—into a certain body cavity.

"Let's do this in the cage," Zane Donahue said.

"Yes, let's!" A regal-looking woman joined us. How I hadn't noticed her before is a mystery, because she was someone you couldn't miss. Tall and substantial, wearing a wide-brimmed hat of robin's-egg blue and a flowing dress to match, she appeared to be in her late sixties. Her face was evenly tanned. Her sunglasses were the size of coffee can lids. She wore white gloves, and the bracelets on her arms jangled like wind chimes.

"You are mar-ve-lous!" she said, looking right at me. "I want to see this. Spare no expense, Zane."

"I won't, Princess," Zane Donahue said. "What do you say, boys?"

Die Scum was nodding his head.

"Not interested," I said.

"But you must!" Princess said, reaching out to touch my chest.

Die Scum issued another curse. Princess turned to him, put a finger to her lips, and he shut up.

"Mike," Zane Donahue said, "let me present to you Princess Moira Montenegro."

She smiled and held out her hand like I should kiss it. I just shook it and said, "Your highness?"

Princess Moira held my hand firmly. "I have faith in you already," she said.

"Let's do this!" Die Scum said.

"I'm not going to fight," I said.

He called me a name that began with *chicken*.

"No call for that!" Princess Moira said. "You will not speak unless spoken to."

Die Scum rolled his eyes. But he didn't speak.

"Now then," Zane said, "let's put this on the line. Three rounds, fifty grand purse."

"No!" said Princess Moira. "One hundred. Guaranteed!"

"Now we're talking," Zane Donahue said.

"We're not talking," I said.

"Why don't we step into my office?" Zane Donahue said.

W hen he closed his office door, I said, "That was a high school production of *The Glass Menagerie*."

"Excuse me?" Donahue said. He went to his flight-deck-sized desk and picked up a dark-wood humidor.

"Clumsy drama," I said.

Donahue shook his head. "Speak plainly."

"You set that up," I said.

He smiled and opened the humidor, held it out to me. I looked at the harem of dusky beauties inside it, and shook my head.

Donahue took out a cigar, closed the humidor and placed it back on the desk. As he reached for his cutter he said, "I want to hire you." He snipped the end of his cigar.

"I'm already employed," I said.

He picked up a silver lighter that was next to the humidor and clicked it. A bluish butane flame whooshed out. He held the cigar end over the flame, turning the stogie delicately. Then he closed the lighter and took a couple of starter puffs. He looked at the end of the cigar and blew gently on it, making sure it was perfectly lit.

"You work part time for a lawyer," Donahue said. "And spend the rest of your time watching seaweed hit the beach."

"You'd be surprised how well that pays," I said. "All the starfish kick in."

"I'm serious, Romeo. Sit."

I sat in a big leather chair. Zane Donahue sat in another big leather chair. Everything was big in his office, including his cigar.

"Why won't you consider fighting for me?" Donahue said. "That hundred grand is real cash money."

"I'm not a violent person," I said.

Donahue snorted. "I know your cage record. Funny, but I can't find anything before that."

"Nothing funny about it," I said.

"You are apparently a man with a past. And you don't want anybody to know about it."

"Life can only be understood backward," I said. "But it must be lived forward."

"You come up with that?"

"Kierkegaard."

He took a languid pull on his cigar and let the smoke issue from his mouth like a genie from a lamp. "A fighter who reads Kierkegaard. You are going to make a lot of money."

"Where do your fights take place? Are you licensed?"

"No need for that. They take place on the open sea."

I narrowed my eyebrows accusingly. It's an art.

"Do you know anything about the old gambling ships in L.A.?" Zane Donahue said.

"A way to beat the anti-gambling ordinances," I said. "No jurisdiction out at sea."

"It was a heckuva system till Earl Warren, the governor, decided to shut the operation down. He did it by manipulating the law."

"What law?"

"Nuisance law. Can you imagine that? Gambling aboard a ship was a nuisance! I tell you, the law is an ass."

"Mr. Bumble said that," I said.

"Who?"

"In *Oliver Twist*."

Flicking cigar ash into a glass ashtray set inside a leather container sitting on the corner of his desk, Donahue said, "We go out twenty-five miles, past Coast Guard jurisdiction, a pleasure cruise. Make a day of it. Get back close to midnight."

"And you have fights?"

"Two," he said. "An undercard and a main event."

"And who watches these fights?"

"People with money, of course." Zane Donahue smiled. "They become rabid fans. Like the princess. Now what's she going to do with all her money if not have fun with it? And she just loves you, I can tell."

"She's not subtle," I said.

"She has a good eye for talent and what makes a good show," he said.

"I'm not in show business," I said.

"We're all in show business," Donahue said. "There's no such thing as a private life anymore. You either control your own show, or somebody's going to control it for you."

"You make a good case for going back to the nineteenth century," I said.

"Is that where you'd like to be, Mike?"

"With a little homestead on the lone prairie."

He rested his cigar on the deep impression in the glass ashtray. He picked up his phone and made a few swipes.

"I assume," he said, looking at the phone, "that your answer is firm?"

"It is."

"I'm a determined guy," he said. "I usually get my way."

"It's good for the soul to be disappointed every once in awhile."

"Who says I have a soul?" said Zane Donahue. "Thanks for stopping by, Mr. Romeo."

I was walking back to my Corona when somebody said, "Hey, Mike!"

It was a blast from my past. Archie Jennison and I had done cage time together twelve years earlier. Time had not been good to him. He looked like Mickey Rourke's uglier brother.

He pumped my hand and smiled. He was missing a front tooth. His eyes had a puffy, drunk look.

"Man, it's good to see you here," Archie said. "You coming on board?"

"Board?"

"One of the fighters."

I shook my head. I gave the party a quick scan for Die Scum. He was on the far side of the yard, huddling with Princess Moira. I was glad they were far away.

Archie said, "It's good money."

"It's a young man's game, Arch. What are you now?"

"Only the big four-oh, last August." He stuck out his hairy chest. I think I was the only guy by the pool with a shirt on. "Go ahead, hit me."

"I'll pass," I said.

"Mike, there's all sorts of miracle working juice now. You can go till you're seventy."

"You have a fall-back plan?" I asked.

He smiled. "You know me, Mike. Only one way to fight and live, and that's just bull ahead, make money, enjoy yourself. Otherwise you might as well work at a bowling alley in South Dakota."

"There are some very nice people in South Dakota," I said.

"Same old Mike! You always had funny things to say."

"Sometimes I even get serious."

He put his arm around me. "I'm kind of glad to hear you say that. You think we could talk?"

"Aren't we talking now?"

"I mean, you know, quietly."

"Sure," I said.

"How bout now?"

"Now?"

"There's a place I know," he said. "Got something I want to run by you."

"You're not selling life insurance, are you?"

"Nah!"

"Amway?"

"Come on, man. I'll buy you a friendly drink."

"If you put it that way."

"Bosco!" he said.

"What?"

"Bosco. It's just a thing I say."

"I guess everybody's got to have a thing they say."

He laughed. "What's yours?"

I showed him the tattoo on my left forearm. *Vincit Omnia Veritas.*

"Oh yeah, I remember that," he said. "I forgot what it means."

"Truth conquers all things," I said.

"Heavy," he said.

"Some days I even believe it."

I followed Archie's Volvo in my classic Mustang convertible, Spinoza. We came to a little place in Venice, a hipster bar, built in the 1930s and now redone for the twenty-somethings who thought they were the first generation to appreciate Irish whiskey. The dark wood paneling gave the interior an old-school appearance, like a speakeasy.

We sat at the bar, which went around in a rectangular shape. A young, female bartender in a white shirt and black vest came over. Archie ordered a double Bushmills Black. I called a Smithwick's pint.

"It sure is good to see you again, Mike," Archie said in that big, welcoming voice I remembered.

"Let me ask you something, Arch."

"Anything, man."

"Did you know I was going to be at Donahue's party?"

He didn't answer.

"Arch?"

A big grin. "Okay, you got me. I did. Zane told me. He knew we fought together. He knows a lot. And he's a good man to have on your side."

The bartender set down our drinks.

Archie lifted his glass. "May ye live to be a hundred, with one year extra to repent!"

We clinked and drank. Archie took in his whole shot and motioned to the bartender for another.

"Ah, the good old days," he said. "When was the last time we were together? Memphis?"

"I think so, yeah."

"You were so good," Archie said. "I always wanted to ask you where you trained."

"I picked things up along the way," I said.

"Didn't you have a teacher, a trainer?"

"Sure. A couple. And books."

"Books?" Archie said. "You can't learn to fight from books."

"Who says?"

Archie shook his head. "You serious?"

"You look at the pictures and you practice."

The bartender put another shot of Bushmill's in front of Archie, who said, "So what did you do before you went into fighting?"

"You're stalling," I said.

He downed his shot. "Zane says you're some kind of investigator now."

"I do some work for a lawyer. I'm not licensed for private stuff, if that's what you're thinking."

"That's what I'm thinking," he said.

A skinny guy in a porkpie hat, with a red ascot around his throat, shoved some change into a classic jukebox. A moment later the place was filled with a Celtic jig.

"Tell me why you want an investigator," I said.

"Not just anybody. It has to be somebody I trust."

"You pay an investigator, you buy their trust."

"But I know I can trust you. We were brothers once. The word back then also was you were a straight-up guy."

"What's your issue?"

"Nothing much," he said. "Just that somebody wants to kill me."

I waited for him to explain.

"The last month I been getting 'em," he said. "Voicemails from a private number. Whispering voice saying 'Don't stick your nose in any further.' A couple of notes in my mailbox. Same stuff."

"Those exact words?"

"More or less."

"What is it you're supposed to be sticking your nose in?" I said.

Archie motioned for another Bushmill's.

"How many of those are you going to pound?" I said.

"As many as it takes to get through this," he said.

On and on went the Celtic jig.

Archie got his drink but this time he decided to nurse it. He took a small sip and said, "Ever hear of the Hollywood Hunk murder?"

"Rings a bell," I said. "Back in the nineties, wasn't it?"

"January 8, 1996. Young wannabe actor named Shad Halls. Jogger spotted his body. Half of it, anyway. The upper half, with no head on it. Head was found a little way off, propped on a rock. Also, his guts were missing."

"Yeah, it's coming back."

"Never found who did it. It was sort of like that other case, from way back. The one with the girl, what was it?"

"The Black Dahlia," I said.

Archie nodded. "Anyway, there were a couple of guys the cops suspected in the Hunk case. A porn actor was the prime suspect, he and Shad Halls were together for awhile. Meanwhile, the cops questioned some other people, one guy was a vet. I mean, a veterinarian, respected guy, guy who saves dogs and cats. He may have had some connection to Halls, too, through a pet store or something, where Halls used to work. But that's it, so the cops double down on the porn actor, a guy who called himself Woody Wildman."

I shook my head at the decline of civilization.

"So anyway," Archie said, "this vet leaves town a few months later, goes off to Europe somewhere, never comes back. Nobody knows why. Maybe he didn't like the way he was handled by the cops and all that. He hates America. Something. Anyway, he's off the radar for years, and finally dies somewhere in Finland."

"What happened to Mr., um, Wildman?"

"AIDS," Archie said. "And the cops cleared him before he died."

"Nice of them," I said.

"So a year ago some new evidence turns up. A stash of pictures of Shad Halls in, you know, nothing. Black-and-white pictures, sort of artistic, if that's your idea of artistic."

"Not Ansel Adams, is what you're saying."

"Am I?" Archie said. "Who is Anvil Adams?"

"Go on with your story," I said.

Archie took another sip of Irish whiskey. "Okay. Turns out these pics are kind of in a style that this veterinarian was into. He did photography on the side, for fun and sometimes money, of actors and things. So these pictures are a link between Shad Halls and the vet."

"Not a very strong link for murder," I said. "Maybe the vet didn't take the pictures."

"Except for one thing," Archie said. "They were found in a box underneath the vet's house, in a hiding place."

"Okay, now you're talking evidence. So what's your interest in all this?"

"I'm the guy who found the box," Archie said.

"How'd you happen to do that?"

"I grew up in that house," he said.

"What?"

He nodded. "The vet was my father."

I raised my eyebrows. I'm subtle that way.

Archie said, "Heavy, isn't it?"

"Have you gone to the police with this evidence?"

He finished his drink. He started to motion for another. I caught his arm and pulled it down.

"Just talk," I said.

"I was gonna go to the cops," he said. "But somebody stole the pictures."

"How?"

"Broke into my place. Took 'em."

"Just the pictures?"

"Nah, some other stuff, too. They were in a box, like I said, so maybe the guy figured it had something valuable in it."

"Hard to buy that," I said.

"How come?"

"Burglars look for obvious value. Jewelry, laptops. They don't mess with ambiguous things."

"You think somebody knew what was in the box?" Archie said.

"Did you tell anybody you had these?" I said.

"Nobody, that's the thing. And then phone calls started. Private numbers, guy warning me not to say anything to anybody."

"About the box?"

"That's all he'd say. I'm sure that's what he means." He shook his head, looking at his empty glass. "Can I have one more, Mike?"

"Drinking problem, maybe?"

"Come on."

"I'm not your mother," I said. "But I haven't seen you for twelve years and now, out of the blue, you find me and give me this incredible story all while soaking yourself in whiskey."

"You think I'm lying about all this?"

"I don't know what to think," I said. "But it doesn't quite pass the schnoz test."

"The what?"

"The schnozzola. The nose. I used to do some work with a PI named Joey Feint, and he had the schnoz test. He knew when something didn't smell quite right. My schnoz is tingling now. Which means there's something you're not telling me."

He took a long moment to think it over, tapping his empty glass on the bar top.

"You really are good," he said.

"Come clean," I said.

A few more taps. I put my hand over his to stop it. His knuckles were gnarled from years of pounding.

"Okay, okay," he said. "I got some other troubles."

"Why am I not surprised?"

"Girl troubles."

"Go on."

"She's twenty-three."

I put my forehead in my hand.

"I know!" Archie said.

"You're almost twenty years older," I said.

"So?"

"These things usually don't end well," I said. "She live with you?"

He nodded.

"What's her name?"

"Missy. Missy Nolan."

"So what's the trouble?" I said.

"Drugs."

"Oh, this keeps getting better," I said.

"She is in with some bad people."

"Shocker."

"I'm having another drink, I don't care." Archie called out to the bartender. He was starting to get loud.

I fished out one of Ira's lawyer cards. "Here. You go to the cops and you tell them what you've told me, about the pictures. And you better tell them about any trouble you're in. You may need some legal counsel. This is the lawyer I work for."

The bartender brought Archie another shot. He looked at it like a sad slosh. Which is what he was.

"I'm scared, Mike," he said. "I mean, you find out your father was maybe a killer, and now people are warning me not to say anything."

"What about your girlfriend?" I said. "Aren't you scared for her?"

"Well, yeah, sure."

"I can just hear the tremble in your voice," I said.

"What are you saying?"

I tapped my nose. "What aren't you telling me?"

He downed the drink in one knock. "Maybe this was a bad idea," he said.

"Maybe it was."

"I thought I could talk to you."

"That's what you've been doing."

My phone buzzed. It's a white-list phone, programmed by Ira. He's clever that way.

It was Artra Murray, a doctor who lives near me in Paradise Cove. She runs a public medical clinic off Pacific Coast Highway.

"Just thought you should know your friend C Dog is here," she said.

C Dog referred to Carter "C Dog" Weeks, a twenty-something musician I was trying to get off a weed habit and into good health.

"What's wrong?" I said.

"He'll live," Artra said. "But he wondered if you could come in."

"On my way."

I put the phone down. "Look, Arch. Tell the cops about the

phone calls. California has anti-stalking laws, including by cell phone, so if you report it your carrier can set it up so if you ever ID the other guy's carrier, you can get a subpoena for their records."

"That's good stuff, Mike."

"It's a long shot, but that's the only kind of shot you have right now. And you're going to have to settle up with the drug dealers. I'd get your girlfriend out of town until you do. Maybe permanently. Ever think of that?"

"Where would I go?" Archie said.

"South Dakota," I said.

I left Archie with his booze and drove Spinoza down the new incline to PCH. The sky was blue and the sun friendly. A stiff wind whipped the waters of the Pacific, turning it into a blanket of white caps. It was the perfect picture of the city I was gradually calling home. Always something churning on the surface, and underneath all sorts of stuff you can't see.

It was a fifteen-minute drive up the coast to Artra's clinic. The clinic was set back on the inland side of the highway, behind a strip mall.

Artra Murray had been the first African-American woman appointed head of surgery at Johns Hopkins. She gave up a lucrative professional practice several years ago to bring medical services to the poor. She lives modestly in her double-wide in Paradise Cove and is at the clinic six days a week.

She has more energy than most women half her age, which is sixty-five. That's why I wasn't surprised to find her refilling the paper cup dispenser at the Sparkletts water cooler near the front desk.

"Major surgery?" I said.

She looked over her shoulder at me. "You talking about the cups or our friend Carter?"

"Let's start with C Dog. I can always get a drink of water later."

Now she faced me. She was wearing a white smock over blue scrubs. Her hair was gray and stylish. She looked like she'd be perfectly at home hosting a tea as she would asking for a scalpel.

"Let me put it this way," Artra said. "His problems are behind him."

"Uh-oh," I said. "Thrombosis of the hemorrhoid, perhaps?"

She laughed. "Where did you pick that up?"

"Reading," I said. "Can I perform his surgery?"

"Sure," Artra said. "I'll get the butcher knife and bottle of rye, and you can go right to work."

"Done."

"But that's not what's bothering our friend," Artra said. "What entered into his backside was a genus of the Cactaceae family."

"Cactus?"

She nodded.

"C Dog fell in some cactus?" I said.

"Not exactly fell. More like sat on."

I winced. "How did he manage that?"

"Maybe you should ask him that yourself."

C Dog was in a bed in a cubicle, looking sadder than a mutt without a supper dish. Carter Weeks had the lean body of the former drug user slash rock musician he fancied himself to be.

"So what's this I hear about some prickly behavior?" I said.

"Aw, man." C Dog's wild thatch of blond hair framed his sad face.

"You're going to have to tell me," I said.

"Why?"

"For the betterment of mankind. We don't want this happening to anybody else."

"Just ... don't."

"Were you high?" I said.

"No!" He tossed his head back. "I swear! I'm clean, going on two months."

"Okay," I said. "Then what are cactus needles doing where sun rarely shines?"

He sighed. "I was playing Freak with some buds."

"Freak?"

"Kind of like keep away, only extreme. You play it with a Frisbee. In the hills."

"Uh-huh. Where does the cactus come in?"

"Total accident."

"But how? Did it tear through your pants?"

He didn't answer.

"Please tell me you were wearing pants," I said.

He looked away.

I said, "You were playing this game in the buff?"

"That's why it's called Freak."

There are times in life when you are presented with a set of facts that strain your optimism for the future of mankind.

"So you are telling me you ran around after a Frisbee in the snake-and-cactus infested hills of Malibu, dingling and dangling, and you were not high?"

"I swear!"

"Now that is even more troubling than if you'd *been* high."

He put out his hands, pleading. "Come on, man, haven't you ever done anything crazy?"

"Not where the tender parts of my body are concerned," I said.

C Dog closed his eyes.

"The main thing," I said, "is to learn from disaster. Experience is an expensive lesson, Benjamin Franklin said. But the only way to grow wisdom."

"Benjamin Franklin can kiss my—"

"Don't finish that sentence." I dragged a chair over to his bedside and sat. "Franklin left us many a fine aphorism."

"A fine what?"

"Short, wise saying. Plough deep while sluggards sleep and you shall have corn to sell and to keep."

"What does that even mean?"

"You've got to expand your mind, C. Here's another one. He who exposes his butt to needles should not complain when the point is made."

He shook his head. His eyes were completely vacant.

"That last one I just made up," I said. "But you can't deny the wisdom of it now, can you?"

Half smile from C. I considered that a partial victory.

"How many beers did you have?" I said.

The smile vanished. "Come on, man, I just wanted to have some fun with my friends."

"Is this fun?"

He tugged on his ear.

"C, listen to me now, you're off to a good, new start. Don't let one little bump in the road, as it were, get you off track."

"Life sucks."

"We've got to work on your vocabulary," I said. "I think it needs to be a tad more expressive."

"Man, would you talk like a normal person sometimes?"

"Alenda lux ubi orta libertas."

"What the h—"

"It means light is to be nourished where liberty abounds."

"What the h—"

"It means that with your freedom, seek light, not mere pleasure."

"I don't know what the—"

"Now you get some rest and do what the doc tells you. We'll do some more philosophical training when you get out."

"Yeah?"

I nodded. "You're going to be a stand-up guy from now on."

He closed his eyes.

"Now," I said. "Tell me the real reason you wanted to see me."

. . .

"I got a little bit of a problem," C Dog said.

"Continue."

"Promise not to get mad?"

"I will only promise that I won't spank you on the backside," I said. "That would be cruel."

After a long sigh, he said, "You know, you scare me sometimes."

"I sometimes scare myself," I said. "Don't let that stop you."

He looked at the ceiling as if searching for an escape hatch. Not finding one, he said, "I owe some money to a guy, and he wants it. And I don't have it."

What was it about me today? Archie's girlfriend and now C Dog, owing.

I said, "If this is about drugs—"

"Not!" C Dog said.

"What kind of money are we talking about?"

"Kind of a lot."

"Be specific for me."

He paused. Then, looking at the palms of his hands, he said, "Twenty thou."

I sat back in my chair.

"I take it," I said, "this is not a legitimate lender to whom you owe this money."

"No, man."

"Explain."

"Okay, you're gonna find out anyway. You always do."

I made a *come on* motion with my hand.

"I needed some big money," C Dog said. "About six months ago I found a guy who would give it to me. Fifteen grand."

"Who was this guy?"

"His name is Truman."

"Like the president?"

"Which president?"

"The one named Truman," I said.

"There was a president named Truman?"

"Yes."

"What was his last name?"

I kept myself from slapping my forehead. "What was the money for?"

"My band. Equipment, speakers. We need it to go to the next level."

"As I recall, your band is named Unopened Cheese."

"Yeah."

"What level are you at now?"

"Pretty low. But not for long."

"So you found this guy. A loan shark, right? And now you're behind and owe twenty, with penalty and interest."

"I guess so."

"You *guess* so?"

"But it was for my band, man."

"Oh, thank goodness. For a second there I thought you were crazy and stupid. I didn't know you were a legitimate businessman."

C Dog pressed his thin lips together.

I said, "So where is the equipment?"

He closed his eyes.

"Don't tell me," I said.

"Okay," he said.

"Okay what?" I said.

"Okay I won't tell you."

"Where's the money?" I said.

"You said not to tell you."

"He took it all?"

"No, man, I'm not that stupid. Only half."

"Half stupid?"

"No! I only gave him half the money."

"Glad that's cleared up. Where's the other half?"

He took a deep breath. "I have about five thou. It's in a duffel bag under my place."

"If my calculations are correct, you spent over two grand of half of fifteen thousand. On what? Equipment?"

C Dog Weeks took a bit of the bed sheet between his fingers and twisted it.

"On what, C?" I said.

"I had a party for the band."

"A two thousand dollar party?"

"Had to rent a place."

"Of course," I said. "You wouldn't want to *waste* that money."

I stood. This one was going to take some pacing around. For some reason unknown to me, Carter "C Dog" Weeks was something of a project with me. Maybe if Ira was grilling me I'd confess that it had something to do with saving myself, vicariously.

But Ira wasn't here.

"Is there anything you can sell?" I asked. "Your car?"

"I can't sell my car!"

"And your guitar."

"Not my guitar, man!"

"Do you want your legs broken? Your fingers? How will you play guitar then?"

And then the animation was gone. C Dog seemed to shrink into his pillow. In another moment he had his head in his hands and wept.

I'm not normally a hair-tousle guy. But C opened up a small suitcase of sympathy inside me, the one I usually keep clasped shut. So I tousled his hair and said, "I'll see about getting you out of here."

In Artra's office, she said, "Have a look around. It may be the last time you see it."

"What?" I said.

"Closing up shop," she said.

"Why?"

"Rent's going up. We're not making it. Budget cuts in Sacramento. We just don't have the cash flow. We're coming up twenty K short a month, at least."

"Don't you have some donors?"

"I can't keep fundraising," she said. "There's too much work to do. Homeless population around here is exploding."

"Good weather," I said.

"Oh, it's a lot more than that. Now you can smoke pot without fear. There's been a thirty percent increase in the homeless in the last six months. Most of them teens or early twenties. They call them marijuana migrants. They get here with no money, no prospects, and the idiotic Board of Supervisors is making sure they all go to the black market."

"I don't follow."

"They put a ten percent levy on medical and recreational marijuana, supposedly to fund building more homeless shelters. But that's raised the cost of legal pot, so the black market still exists."

"Simple economics," I said.

"Stupid politicians," Artra said.

Artra Murray had not only given her toil and tears to this place, but also most of her own funds. The world increasingly needs more people like Artra. But it keeps giving us more people like Die Scum.

Her phone lit up.

"Have to take this," she said. "Will you take Carter back to the Cove?"

"Sure," I said.

"Pick up the rubber donut at the front desk."

Driving back to the Cove I told C Dog, "If you ever do anything like this again, and I'm not talking cactus, I'm talking loan sharks, I will personally give you a guitar enema, you got that?"

"Come on, man."

"And you will not use that word around me."

"What word?"

"*Man*. Only men are allowed to use that word, and you are not a man. You're a mollusk."

"A what?"

"A sea-dwelling snail, an excretion machine, a non-thinking digestive tract. You're not a man."

"Aw, come on ma ... dude."

"I've invested time in you," I said. "It's turning out to be a bad investment."

C Dog looked out at the ocean on our right. Even the back of his head looked confused.

He turned back to me. "Everybody ends up thinking I'm nothin'."

"You're alive," I said. "That's a start. And now you've got a choice. You can stay dumb and soft, like a mollusk, or you can think and work your way back into being a human. Maybe even a man. What'll it be?"

C Dog chewed his lip.

We were coming up to Paradise Cove Road.

"Choose before I make the turn," I said.

"Okay! Yes! I don't even know what it means, but yeah."

"All right then," I said. "Tomorrow I'll go talk to the guy."

His eyes were misty as he looked at me. "Truman?"

"Yeah."

"You can't! He won't."

"I can. He will."

In Los Angeles we call our strip malls "plazas." It lends the places more cachet and hearkens back to California history when fat Dons sunned themselves on their ranchos while exploiting cheap indigenous labor.

And cheap was the look of this particular plaza in Granada Hills. Like so many of its ilk, it did not have a consistent color scheme. Even the word *Plaza* in the big street sign had blue for the *P* and the *z*. The other letters were some kind of off-white.

Fittingly, the most prominent of the stores had a gaudy pink awning with a giant 99¢ in the middle. Next to it was a chiropractor, a discount cigarettes shop, a coin-operated laundry, and a realty office with the *t* missing from its sign. A quick look and you'd think it spelled *Really*. Which is what I was asking myself at just this moment.

The place I was looking for was up on the second level, where they had a suite of offices. Yes, here was a hub of high-end businesses. A travel agency with a couple of faded pictures of river cruises taped to the window. A luggage importer. A sound system repair shop.

And TruSports Memorabilia.

The door was locked. It was glass and inside I could see a dismal outer area with one glass case. Inside the case were some cards, presumably baseball, to make the place look legit.

I tapped on the glass.

A second later a guy who was round and brown, with a black beard and balding head, wearing what had to be a XXX T-shirt with a Philadelphia Eagles logo, came from the back.

"Appointment only," he shouted.

"Can I make an appointment for one minute from now?" I said.

"You have to call."

"I'm calling," I said. "Through the door."

He shook his head.

"It's about the money," I said.

He shrugged.

I said, "Tell Truman if he wants his money he needs to talk to me."

The guy paused. His forehead wrinkled. Then he reached in his pocket and pulled out some keys. He unlocked the door, opened it a crack.

"We don't do business unless you make appointment." He had a slight accent from the Middle-Eastern stew of languages.

"Ah, you think I'm an undercover cop," I said.

"Why would I think that?" he said.

"Because you have that look about you."

"Look?"

"Let's just say you're not going on the cover of *Boys' Life*." I put my shoulder to the door and knocked him back. I stepped inside, closed the door. After a second of being stunned, the guy came at me with a roundhouse right. I caught his fist in my hand and bent his arm back toward his shoulder. Then I had him down on his knees.

He said a bad word.

A guy who looked similar to the fellow on the ground—only in a less rounded shape—appeared from the back. Had to be brothers.

"Hey," the new guy said. "What is this?"

"You Truman?" I said.

He went back from whence he came. I kept holding his twin on the floor. It was what you would call an embarrassing situation.

The other guy came back pointing a revolver at me.

"You don't want to do that," I said. "I'm not here to rob you. And you don't want the cops asking you questions about blood on your floor and all that."

"Let him up," the guy with the gun said.

"I'm assuming you are Truman," I said. "You're the one I want to talk to."

"Let him up."

"If you promise to play nice," I said.

In answer, the guy took a step closer to me with the gun.

I released my grip and stepped back.

"Why don't you get out while you can still walk?" the gun guy said.

"Do you have a Mo Vaughn rookie card?" I asked.

"What?"

"He was my favorite player as a kid. Just wondered if you had one."

The first guy was on his feet now, breathing fast and heavy.

"I am going to give you one chance to say what you want," the guy with the gun said. "And then you are going to get out."

"You want your money, don't you?"

"You did not borrow from us," he said.

"I represent somebody who did. I'm here for friendly negotiations, nothing else. So why don't you put the iron away and we sit down and talk about this, since it benefits both of us."

"Shoot him," the other guy said. "Or let me have some of him."

"I believe you mean a piece of him," I said.

Gun Guy said, "Who you come for?"

"Weeks," I said.

"That guy?" he said with thinly-veiled disgust. "Never should have given him a thing."

"But now you're doing the old shark dance with him," I said. "You're scaring the poor kid."

"Poor kid! Thinks he's a player."

"He's trying to get his life together. I know he owes you money, so let's figure out a way for you to get some of it."

"Some of it? How about the whole thing?"

He still held the gun on me.

"Let me take him apart," the gunless guy said.

"You did not do so good the first time," Gun Guy said. "All right, come into my office. Milo, you wait out here."

Milo did not look like he wanted to wait. As I walked past him I said, "Will you look for that Mo Vaughn rookie card for me?"

He told me where he wanted to shove the card.

"Not the best place to display it," I said.

T he inner office was cramped and messy, with open boxes all around, shelves stuffed with other boxes of various sizes, and the dull white paint job of a state insane asylum. There was a desk with papers all over it and one open KFC box with the remains of a drumstick bone in it.

"Nice filing system," I said.

The guy put his gun in the right-hand drawer of the desk and sat. He didn't offer me a chair. There was no chair to be offered.

"You're Truman?" I said.

"Where is my money?" he said.

"Well, first we have to decide on the settlement amount."

"The amount is twenty. As of today. Anything else?"

"That's not much of a negotiation," I said.

"We do not negotiate. How fast do I get my money?"

"How about five thousand tomorrow?" I said. "Then you forgive the rest of the loan."

Truman snorted. He laced his fingers behind his head, leaned back in his chair. The chair squeaked.

I said, "And also you find me that Mo Vaughn rookie card and I'll pay you double market value for it. Then we call the whole thing square."

"You are a crazy man. What do you think I am running here?"

"An illegal loan operation," I said.

"No," he said, snapping his hands back in front of him. "We do open business, all right? We don't hide the ball, all right? This guy, this Weeks, he comes in and he wants money, and he tells us how he is going to pay us back. And then he does not. Meth head."

"You know this how?"

Truman shrugged.

"Look at it this way, then. A goodwill gesture for someone struggling with an addiction. And also, I won't make any trouble for you."

"You make trouble for me?" He shook his head. "You do not know who you are talking to."

"Truman," I said. "Who was a fine president, by the way."

"I am done talking." He opened the drawer and pulled out the gun again. He held it off to the side. That was the extent of his goodwill gesture.

"You really think you can operate like this?" I said. "What does that say about the state of the world today?"

"Get out."

"You think you can threaten with a gun? And hurt people you lend money to? You think these are Al Capone days?"

"Who?"

"Did you even go to school?"

He raised the gun. "Don't come back. I don't even want to see your shadow."

"This has been just about the worst negotiation I have ever been involved in," I said. "There was one time I tried to talk some Girl Scouts into a discount on cookies, and they wouldn't budge. You are exactly like those Girl Scouts."

I waited until his expression changed. I think he was trying to figure out if I was dangerous or mentally unstable. I like it when people think that way about me.

Something came at me from the side.

Most people don't know you can practice peripheral vision. I used to do that, walking down the streets of New Haven, looking into windows without turning my head. Comes in handy at times like this. For it was Milo giving me the bum's rush.

With a simple back step I let physics do most of the work. Milo threw his right but it whizzed past my chin. I stuck my leg out and pushed his back. He face-planted into the carpet.

"Cut it, Milo!" Truman said.

Milo groaned.

"Get out," Truman said to me.

"You're not going to shoot," I said. "You're a businessman."

He half smiled. I hate half smiles. Commit one way or the other.

"You tell Weeks he has five days to come up with fifteen," Truman said. "Then we will talk about the rest. Now get out or I will risk the blood."

"I'll make an appointment next time," I said.

. . .

R abbi Ira Rosen, Attorney-at-Law, former Mossad agent, lives in a modest home in the Los Feliz district of L.A. He's my only friend in the world. We'd met in Nashville, on the street, when a few young punks sought to rob this middle-aged man in a wheelchair. Ira could have broken every one of their bones, but did not, his morality holding him back.

I did not have such hesitations. When the dust cleared he read me something of a religious riot act. He's been trying to save my soul ever since. He tries to ply me with tea. As usual I refused it, got a bottle of water from the refrigerator, and returned to Ira's office, which is also his living room.

"Man is a ruined experiment," I said, taking a chair.

"Why so cheery today?" Ira said. His soft gray hair was full under his familiar yarmulke. And while his girth is not as slim as it once was, his head and hands were every bit as sharp as when he used them to kill terrorists.

"I find certain people rude," I said.

"Oh no," Ira said, which is something he says a lot in my presence.

"No blood," I said.

"I'm not entirely sure I want to hear about it," Ira said.

"My friend at the beach, C Dog?"

"The would-be rock star."

"He got in some trouble with a loan shark, and I went to him to try to negotiate a deal."

"Now I'm sure I don't want to hear about it," Ira said.

"Then let's talk about torsos," I said.

He raised his eyebrows.

"What do you know about the Hollywood Hunk murder?"

"Oh my, there's a memory flogger," Ira said. "I happen to know a good deal about it."

"Fill me in."

"Well, let's see. As I recall it was a young, good-looking actor who was surgically bisected and gutted, like that Black Dahlia case back in the forties. Also, his head was removed and placed on a rock some yards away from the body. Up near the Hollywood sign. There was a pornographic actor who was a suspect, but was ultimately cleared. And I believe a veterinarian was questioned, too."

"Your mind is like a steel trap," I said.

"Clean living, my friend. Now what's this about?"

"I met up with an old fighting colleague at a party."

"Party?"

"At Zane Donahue's," I said.

Ira shook his head.

"It's all right," I said. "I owe him a favor. Anyway, this guy, Archie Jennison wanted to talk to me and he told me he thinks this vet did it. He found photographs that were supposedly taken by the vet, showing the actor. And then he tells me that the vet was his father."

Ira folded his hands on his stomach. His pondering position. "All this sounds rather incredible. What's he going to do with the photos?"

"Nothing," I said. "They were stolen."

"And I suppose he wants you to try to find them."

I shook my head. "He has other problems. Involving drugs and a girlfriend and dealers."

"Then I'm glad you're not getting involved."

"Me, too," I said. "That's why I gave him your card."

"Michael!"

"Just in case," I said. "I don't think anything will come of it. He's got a drinking problem and who knows how reliable his brain is?"

Ira looked at his watch. "I've got to make a couple of phone calls. Why don't you go for a walk?"

"A walk?"

"To the bookstore."

He had that wry look that goes through me every time.

"She's probably there right now," Ira said.

"How would you know?" I said.

"Because there's extra duty going on," Ira said. "You see, they're closing up shop."

I walked over to Los Feliz where the Argo bookstore was. The store was cold inside, like a tomb. Several customers floated around like talking ghosts, making final purchases, saying goodbye to staff.

One of whom I recognized as he walked by. Studious-looking guy, mid-twenties. He's rung up my purchase of *A Coney Island of the Mind* by Lawrence Ferlinghetti a few months ago.

"Sorry to see you go," I said.

"Yeah," he said.

"Can't make it anymore?" I said.

"Minimum wage hike killed us," he said. The Los Angeles County Board of Supervisors had brought in annual minimum-wage increases.

He said, "We were making about three grand a year. Now we'll lose about twenty-five."

"And the staff all lose their jobs."

"Isn't it great?" he said bitterly.

"What are you going to do next?"

"Starbucks," he said. "Everybody ends up at Starbucks."

I smiled.

"Anything I can show you?" he said. "All books on sale."

"I was wondering if Sophie was here."

"Yeah, I think so. You want me to—"

"I'll find her. Thanks."

My stomach did roller derby inside me. What would it be like when I saw her? Was I going to go all schoolboy?

I started to browse, and wound up at the poetry shelf. This was the very spot where I'd kissed Sophie in one of those moments when you hear an orchestra playing in the clouds. The shelf was half empty now and a couple of volumes lay on their sides like dead soldiers.

The death of a bookstore is not a pretty sight.

I did a little more wandering. The Argo had a couple of old sofas for customers. I grabbed a book at random and decided to park myself for awhile. I sat and looked at the book I'd chosen. It was *The River of Doubt: Theodore Roosevelt's Darkest Journey.* Good. Sounded interesting. And I was a Roosevelt fan as a kid, having read a biography of him when I was nine or ten, admiring his over-coming a sickly and weak childhood to become a man of strength and courage.

At the time I was weak and insecure, too, and wanted to turn myself into a man like Roosevelt someday. It would take death for me to get there.

I was just into the first chapter when I looked up and saw Sophie walking toward me.

For a long moment we looked at each other. She wore a white sweatshirt over her tall, athletic body. Her long, sunset-colored hair draped her shoulders. In the silence, not knowing what to say to each other, she pushed her black-rimmed glasses slightly up her nose, as if getting ready to open me up like a book.

I said, "Read any good biographies lately?"

She smiled slightly. "The last biography I read was of Catherine the Great."

"How great was she?"

"Pretty darn great, if length of reign and number of lovers are the measure."

"Wasn't her real name Sophie?" I said.

She nodded. "Sophie Friederike Auguste von Anhalt-Zerbst-Dornburg, to be exact."

"That's one great name."

The lightness between us lasted for one more second. Then Sophie said, "I owe you an explanation. Can we go somewhere and talk?"

"How about the history section?"

She looked at the floor. "Don't make me laugh. Making me laugh will only make this harder."

"Why don't we take a walk?" I said.

I t was a dry, warm day outside. Traffic on Vermont was busy as usual. We walked toward Hollywood Boulevard.

"Too bad about the store," I said.

She nodded. "The way of all commerce, I suppose." She had her arms folded in front of her, as if chilly.

"What's going to happen to all the inventory?"

"The boss is going to warehouse it and build up the online business."

"And what will you do for part time work?"

"It was part time love," she said.

She stopped and faced me. "I freaked when you beat up Josh."

"I thought maybe that was it. Do you know what happened?"

"Only what he told me."

"You're still seeing him?"

She shook her head. "He had to go to the hospital."

"He forced the issue," I said. "I didn't want to fight him. He had two guys with him. He came after me. And there was a little boy. Josh whapped the hot coffee out of my hand and some of it hit the kid, who started crying."

We were near a bus stop, standing under a tree. A European white birch. *Betula pendula.* A hearty breed that can stand up to city stress.

"Did you have to put him in the hospital?"

"I punched him once," I said.

"He was hemorrhaging. He could have died."

"Did he?"

Mr. Sympathy, that's me.

A bus growled up to the stop. Sophie turned toward it. For a second I thought she was going to get on.

We just stood there until the bus spat out a couple of passengers, and an older woman got on.

When the bus pulled away, Sophie said, "Can we go somewhere and sit?"

There was a taco stand across the street with four outside tables with red umbrellas. Two men in work clothes were happily noshing at one of the tables. Sophie headed for the one near the driveway into the parking lot.

She slid onto one of the benches. The salsa music piping out of a bullhorn speaker was in sharp contrast to the mood at our table.

"Can I at least buy you a taco?" I said, as I sat across from her.

"I don't want anything," she said.

She folded her hands on the table. Her fingers were tight. "My father was—is, I guess, still—a filmmaker. Independent. My mom works in administration at Loyola Marymount. They're divorced. When I was a kid my dad developed a coke habit and started hitting my mom."

It took a lot of effort for her to get that out. She kept looking at her hands.

"I just can't be around that," she said.

"Is that why you broke things off with Josh?"

She shook her head. "He never did anything like that. There were other reasons."

"Reason," I muttered.

"Hm?" She looked at me then.

"I was just thinking," I said. "Reason is something I believe in. I try to operate by it. But ..."

"Yes?"

"Sometimes it goes right out the window. Flies away like a bat."

She frowned, waited for me to go on.

"When I kissed you," I said, "I wasn't thinking. I didn't want to think. I just wanted to kiss you."

"If you'd thought about it," she said quietly, "would you have?"

"No," I said.

"And what does *that* mean?"

"It means I can't let myself get close to anybody. It's not fair."

"Fair?"

"I have a friend, lives right around here."

"Yes, I know. The rabbi. Ira. I brought you some books there once."

"I remember," I said. "I remember everything about you from the first moment I saw you."

The gold flecks in her brown eyes made them almost glow. I wanted to kiss her again right there. But I had to be Odysseus lashed to the mast.

"Ira says trouble has a way of finding me," I said. "He's right. I don't go looking for it. I didn't want anything to do with your boyfriend."

"But you hurt him," she said. "Badly."

"That happens," I said. "It's happened in my past and it's going to happen in my future. So it's best that you don't want to see me again."

"But I—" She stopped herself. "At least you're honest."

"I'll be honest about something else," I said.

She waited.

"I wouldn't have missed that kiss for anything in the world," I said.

She put her hand on my arm then. The warmth of her touch went up to my shoulder. The music piping and a car honking sounded like the last note of a crazy urban symphony.

Then Sophie lifted her hand from my arm and said, "I should be getting back to the store."

She stood.

I stood.

"Can I walk you back?" I said.

She looked like she was going to say something. She shook her head.

And turned.

And walked away.

T he next morning I went for a swim.

      To some, the Pacific Ocean in winter is cold. To others, it's bracing. To still others, it's a way to boost the immune system.

To me, it's just wet. But a good way to work out.

When I got back to my towel, C Dog was waiting for me.

"What's up, man?" he said.

"What did I tell you about that *man* stuff?" I said.

"Did you talk to Truman?"

I rubbed the towel on my head. "He's not in much of a forgiving mood."

"So what do I do?"

"Pay him."

"What?"

"It's what you signed up for."

"I haven't got enough money!"

"You can always move to South Dakota."

C Dog spun around in a circle, just like an actual dog looking for a spot to lie down.

"Consequences," I said. "Time you learned about them."

He found his spot and sat heavily on the sand. And said, "Ow!" when he did.

I sat next to him.

"Truman gave me a little information about you," I said.

"What?"

"He called you a meth head."

C Dog's eyes rolled like the mighty ocean.

"Well?" I said.

"No! I don't!"

"Never?"

"A long time ago, but I got away from it fast. It'll fry your brain."

"You deal?"

"Me?"

"You."

He pounded his fist in the sand.

"I take that as a yes," I said.

"Only one time," he said. "Never again."

I grabbed a handful of his T-shirt. "Did you hear what you just said?"

"Huh?"

"Never again. You say something like that, make sure you mean it. Do you mean it?"

"Well ... yeah."

"Not good enough. Say, 'Yes, I mean it.' "

His mouth moved, his chin trembled.

"This is your moment, C," I said. "If you don't say it, we part ways."

"Yes," he said. "I mean it."

"Good," I said, releasing his shirt. "You have taken the oath of the Kalahari."

"The what?"

"It's one of the most ancient oaths in the world, and the most solemn." Boy, I could sound good when I wanted to. "Once you take that oath, you can't go back on it, or the curse of the Kalahari will be upon your tongue. Plus, I'll give you a taste of my own, personal displeasure. We clear?"

"You scare me sometimes."

"Good," I said. "Fear is a great motivator. That money you said's in a duffel bag? Give it to me."

"What are you gonna do with it?"

"Give it back to Truman."

"You're jokin'."

"Do I look funny to you?"

"No way," C Dog said. "That's one big thing you don't look like."

. . .

I left C Dog to contemplate the Kalahari. I showered and shaved and was about to start on the Norton Critical Edition of *Moby-Dick* when my burner phone buzzed. It was Ira Rosen, Attorney-at-Law.

"Meet me at the Pacific LAPD station in an hour," he said.

"What's this about?" I said.

"We're interviewing a potential client. He's being held there."

"A real client?" I said. "What's the charge?"

"Murder."

"Juicy," I said.

"It's your friend," Ira said.

"What?"

"Archie Jennison."

"He's dead?"

"No, charged. They say he killed his girlfriend."

I got in my best investigator clothes—clean blue jeans, a Tommy Bahama Hawaiian shirt, and a light-brown corduroy jacket, and hopped on Pacific Coast Highway.

The morning was overcast, the sea placid, the gulls and pelicans out in force. I was trying to process the idea that Archie had murdered his girlfriend. It was a little bit of a shock to my system. But I couldn't say I was surprised. I hadn't seen Archie in years. What I had seen in our last visit was a guy under some heavy stress who handled it with alcohol.

It was no great leap to conceive of him getting into a drunken rage with a woman a couple decades younger than himself, and doing this deed. When I'd known him back in the day he was an unmoored cannon among a bunch of loose ones.

I took Ocean Avenue through Santa Monica, one of the more desired places to live in L.A., mainly because of proximity to the beach. The downside is you have to actually live there. Expensive and crowded, by turns snooty and tolerant—unless the ones you're supposed to be tolerant of happen to camp near your residence. Then everybody becomes Clint Eastwood saying, "Get off my lawn."

At Venice Boulevard I took a left, then a right on Centinela, then a left on Culver. I parked in front of the station. It had taken me exactly fifty-eight minutes to get there from the Cove. Ira would be proud.

I met Ira inside at the desk. As usual when he was out and about, Ira was using his forearm crutches instead of his wheelchair.

"There's an interview room waiting for us," he said. "I've been told our client is quite distraught."

"Is he sober?" I said.

"Let's find out."

A humorless, buffed-out uniform escorted us into the innards of the station. His name was *Sneed* and he looked like he spent all his off hours working out. I'm all for it. Cops who look like that are more likely to inspire respect than those with a pronounced gut.

But a little humor would've been nice.

He directed us to a plain, white room with a desk and three chairs. There was a clock on the wall. Other than that, it could have been a holding room for somebody in a straitjacket.

A minute later another two officers brought Archie in. He was dressed in his own clothes and they had him in handcuffs. His face was red and blotchy. We made eye contact for a second, then he looked away.

Ira requested the handcuffs be taken off. This was done, and Archie threw himself down in a chair.

"Fifteen minutes," one of the officers said, and with that he closed the door.

"Mr. Jennison?" Ira said.

"Ahhh, she's dead!" Archie said. "What am I gonna do?"

"Easy," Ira said.

"It's crazy, man! I didn't do it!"

"All right," Ira said in his calm, rabbinical voice. "Let's take this one bit at a time. Do you want me to represent you?"

"Sure," Archie said.

"Have you got the money to pay for a lawyer?"

He had to think about it. "Yeah."

"You can have a public defender if you don't."

"No, no, I want you. I want you and Mike."

Ira looked at some notes he'd made on a yellow legal pad. "Your girlfriend's name was Missy Nolan?"

Archie nodded.

"Were you with her yesterday?"

He shook his head.

"But she lived with you, didn't she?"

He nodded.

"But you're saying you weren't with her yesterday?"

"Oh yeah, in the morning. Then I went out."

"When did you see her next?" Ira said.

"I didn't. I ..." Archie put his head in his beefy hands and rubbed his face.

Ira said, "Need some water?"

Archie shook his head.

"All right then," Ira said. "Tell me where you were, what you were doing, from yesterday morning until you got arrested."

After a deep breath, Archie said, "I went to work out at the gym. L.A. Fitness. Got there about nine-thirty."

"You have a membership card? They check you in?"

"What? Yeah, yeah, they do."

"So if we go to that gym and ask them to check the records, it will show you were there?"

Archie frowned. "Yeah. That's what I'm saying."

"Go on," Ira said.

"I'm there about two hours," Archie said. "I showered up then got some lunch."

"Where?"

Archie looked at me. "Don't laugh," he said.

"Why would I laugh?" I said.

"Wendy's," he said. "Not exactly health food."

"Burgers are good for the soul," I said.

"If I can break into the theology discussion," Ira said, with a glance of annoyance at me. "Would there be anyone at Wendy's who could say you were there?"

"I don't know. You know those places. In, out, lots of people."

"Do you have a receipt?" Ira said.

Archie looked surprised at the question. "Why would I? I didn't think I was gonna be ..." He brought a massive fist down on the table. It would have crushed a guy's skull.

"Easy," I said.

"She's dead!"

"Keep your voice down," Ira said. "Anything they hear out there is admissible."

Archie looked at his hands, opened and closed them like he was squeezing invisible rubber balls.

"Where did you go after lunch?" Ira said.

Archie had to think about it. "I drove around. I stopped at some places. I don't know. Then I went to a friend's house and we had some beer and watched some fights."

"This friend have a name?"

"Of course he has a name!" Archie said. "What's the point of all this?"

Ira said, "We need to establish where you were."

"Look," Archie said, "I didn't go back to the apartment at all, okay? Missy and me we had a little fight. Over nothing."

"Fights are always over something," I said.

"I don't even remember," Archie said. "I just got out. And stayed out."

"According to the police report," Ira said, "a preliminary medical exam says Missy Nolan died in the early morning hours, maybe one or two a.m. If you weren't at home, where were you?"

He took in a deep breath. "I was with somebody else."

"A woman?"

He nodded.

I shook my head.

"What's her name?" Ira said.

"We really have to involve her?" Archie said.

"What do you think?" Ira said.

I was looking at Archie's face, trying to read it. Was he so grief-stricken he was being this dim? Or was it his natural state?

"She's kind of fragile right now," Archie said.

"Oh, cry me a river," I said.

Ira snapped a look at me.

"Let's just hold it together," Ira said. "The both of you. Tell me why she's fragile?"

Archie said, "She's trying to stay clean. From horse. Been a month out of detox."

"How old is she?"

"I don't know," Archie said. "Maybe twenty."

I rolled my eyes.

"Are you having a sexual relationship with this woman?" Ira asked.

"Sort of."

"What does that even mean?" I said. "Listen, you—"

Ira raised his hand at me. To Archie, he said, "You spent the night with this woman?"

Archie nodded.

Oh, this was going to be a cakewalk. A recovering heroin addict barely out of her teens, who Archie was using as a sex toy, was his one way out.

"Her name?" Ira said.

"Tirzah," he said.

"A fine Hebrew name," Ira said. "Means, 'she is my delight.' She better be yours, Mr. Jennison. What's her address?"

He gave it to us.

Then threw back his head and wailed.

"Easy," I said.

"Don't tell me that!" Archie jumped to his feet, the chair scraping the floor behind him.

He started for the door.

I got up and put myself in front of him. "Sit down, Arch."

Instead of taking my sane advice, Archie Jennison threw a big, roundhouse left at my dome. Ducking the punch, I tried to grab his arm and get him in a lock, but he was ready for me.

And all of a sudden I'm fighting a madman in a police interview room.

Archie feinted at me with two jabs, then tried a cross-over leg takedown. I reversed him and did a one-eighty, got behind and put on a choke hold. Archie kicked out, thumped the door with his foot, but I had him in control.

The door swung open and Officer Sneed came in.

"I think the interview is over," Ira said.

"That went well," I said. Ira and I were at his van, which was parked on Culver. It had taken three cops and me to get Archie shackled and marched back to his holding cell. In a couple of hours they'd have him shipped downtown by way of a sheriff's bus, to be held in Men's Central Jail.

"Did anything about that bother you?" Ira said.

"How about the whole thing?" I said.

Ira reached in his pocket and handed me some keys. "Archie's," he said.

"How'd you get those?" I said.

"I'm on good terms with these people," Ira said. "They know I could get a warrant. You see, Michael, it pays to be nice to the police. Remember that."

"I'm a puppy dog," I said.

"Like Cerberus you're a puppy dog," Ira said. "Go get a statement from this Tirzah Horrick. We'll meet up later at my house."

"And so the fun begins," I said.

"This one doesn't feel fun at all," Ira said.

Tirzah Horrick lived in an apartment on Arlington Avenue in Crenshaw. The squat, adobe-facade building was next to an alley that faced a giant sign with big red letters. *INJURED IN AN ACCIDENT? Call the Nutter Law Group.*

I thought it would take great confidence to entrust one's accident to a group of nutters.

There was a patchy lawn in the front, a walkway, and two squat Joshua trees on either side, looking like drill sergeants from a tree army. I almost saluted on my way to the entry.

I buzzed her name on the box. A moment later a small voice said, "Yeah?"

"I'm Mike Romeo, working for the lawyer representing Archie. Can we talk?"

"Yeah."

I got buzzed in.

Tirzah Horrick's apartment was on the first floor in the back.

She was waiting for me with the door open. She wore a tank top that was loose on an almost skeletal frame. She had long black hair that hadn't been brushed. Her sunken eyes gave me a scan. Then she took a step to the side and I entered.

The place smelled of last night's pot. The living room had a brown sofa and a red, fake-fur ottoman with two big eyes on it. Would have been somebody's idea of cute when it was new. Now it just looked sad. Or trying to escape. A simple coffee table had the familiar detritus of weed smoking—seeds, ash, glass pipe, Bic lighter, an open package of Oreos, half of them gone from the plastic tray.

"In training?" I asked.

"Huh?" Her voice was thick and her eyes unfocused. "You want somethin' to drink?"

"What have you got?"

"Water."

"I'll pass," I said.

There was a piece of notebook paper on the floor with some writing and a crude, stick-figure cartoon. The cartoon had two boxes with stick figures in them. Above one box it said, *Your Apartment*. Above the other, *My Apartment*. The stick figures in the first box were holding what were apparently major blunts to their faces, as smoke lines went up and also out of their door and through the door of the other box. There was one stick figure in the other apartment, with a talk bubble, saying "Yuck!" And a description underneath, *Your neighbor, the pregnant woman*. At the very bottom of the page, in large letters, was, *PLEASE PUT A TOWEL UNDER YOUR DOOR SO ME AND MY BABY DON'T GET HIGH!*

And then a gray cat jumped onto the sofa and started to pad around, looking at me.

"I need to ask you some questions," I said. "You want to sit down?"

She shrugged and sat on the sofa. The cat made its way to her lap. That left me the choices of the ottoman with the eyes or a chair with a stained cushion.

I chose the ottoman.

"Archie says he was with you on Tuesday night," I said.

"Yeah."

"From when to when?"

"All night."

"I mean, what time did you two first get together?"

"Um." She looked up. "Five o'clock."

"How do you know it was five o'clock?" I said.

She said, "How does anybody know, you know? I saw it. On a clock."

I looked around the place. "Which clock was that?"

"I mean on my phone," she said.

"You checked your phone for the time?"

"Yeah."

"Why did you do that?" I said.

"Because I wanted to know what time it was. Jeez, you ask stupid questions."

"A specialty of mine," I said. "But usually there's a reason we check the time. We have a meeting someplace, or a show is going to start."

"I don't know, okay?" She stroked the cat. "It was five o'clock."

"Exactly five o'clock?"

"Um, yeah."

"Quite a happenstance," I said.

"A what?"

"A coincidence," I said.

"Why don't you talk freakin' English?"

"My failing," I said.

The cat apparently agreed. It jumped off the sofa and left the room.

I said, "How often does Archie come over?"

"I don't know, sometimes."

"What for?"

"What do you mean, what for?"

"Am I not speaking English now?"

"Why don't you just leave it alone? Let me tell it to the cops?"

"Because they won't believe you any more than I do."

She put her palms flat on the sofa, like she was ready to push off. "What does it matter? They can't do nothin' about what I say."

"You'll look like a fool or an accomplice, and Archie will go down. So why don't you tell me where he really was, if you know."

"He was with me!"

"What was he wearing?"

Her eyes glanced off to the side, then came back to me. "You know, what he usually wears."

"He has an injured right hand. Did you notice that?"

"Huh?"

"Hard to miss the bandage around it," I said.

"Yeah, sure, I saw that."

"Right or left hand?"

"Right?"

"No."

"Left!"

"No."

"What?"

"His hand isn't injured," I said.

This brought forth from her small mouth a big, bad word.

"Why are you lying for him?" I said.

"I don't want to talk to you anymore. I'm gonna say what I'm gonna say and you can just deal with it."

I shook my head. "We can't suborn perjury."

"Can't what?"

"Can't knowingly put on a witness we know is lying. Archie'll have to come up with a new witness or a new lawyer."

She said, "Why don't you just help him?"

"Why don't you tell me why you're lying for him."

She tried to cut me up with her glare.

And then we heard squealing tires outside her window. A car door slammed. And a man's voice shouted, "Tirzah!"

"Who's that?" I said.

Tirzah stayed on the sofa. Her eyes were closed.

"My boyfriend," she said.

"How many boyfriends do you have?" I said.

"Just one ... I mean, two."

"Can you tell him to come back later?" I said.

She shook her head. "He doesn't like to be told to do nothin'."

As I tried to parse that sentence, there was a pounding on her door.

"Tirzah!" He pounded on the door again.

I said to her, "You going to answer that?"

"Will you?" she said.

More pounding.

"Why?" I said.

She fell to a prone position on the sofa and pulled a pillow over her ear.

I went over and opened the door.

The guy was about six feet, workout buff. He wore jeans, work boots, and a long-sleeved wool shirt with a red hunting-lodge pattern. He also held a baseball bat in his right hand.

"No game today," I said.

"What ... Who are you?" he said.

"The umpire."

"Where's Tirzah?"

From sofa, Tirzah shouted, "Go away!"

"She wants you to go away," I said.

Bat Boy sized me up. He didn't try the usual hard-guy look. He knew that wouldn't work. This left him hesitant and confused.

"Come on, Tirzah," he said, almost sheepish. "Give him back."

"No!" Tirzah said.

To me he said, "Get out of the way."

"Come back in an hour," I said. "But leave the bat in your car."

Something moved at my feet. A flash of gray.

"Aldo!" Tirzah shrieked.

The gray thing was the cat. It stopped at Bat Boy's feet. He picked it up.

And started walking toward the front doors.

"Stop him!" Tirzah said.

"It's *my* cat," Bat Boy said over his shoulder.

"It isn't!" Tirzah said.

So this is what it had come to. I had a lying witness and a client whose goose was getting nicely basted, and now I was in the middle of a domestic cat dispute.

I should have walked away.

"Hold on," I said to Bat Boy.

"I'm not holdin' nothin'," Bat Boy said, then pushed through the front doors.

I followed him.

Tirzah followed me, hysterically shouting that this was her cat, and that "he's going to sell him for drugs!"

Until I could settle what to do about Tirzah and her testimony, I needed her to calm down.

Bat Boy's truck, a black Chevy pickup, was halfway on the dismal grass that was pretending to be a front lawn.

"Stop now," I said.

He was holding the cat in his left hand and the bat in his right. He opened the cab door with his bat hand and threw the cat in, and closed the door.

Then he turned to face me, putting both hands on the bat and holding it in hitting position.

"Put the bat down," I said.

Tirzah screamed, "Give me back my cat!"

"It's *my* cat!" Bat Boy screamed back.

"If it is your cat," I said, "you can file suit. What you're doing now is robbery. You can go to the joint for that."

"No way," Bat Boy said.

"And it's also a crime to wield that bat."

"Do what?"

"Wield that bat."

"What's that mean?"

"Wield?"

"Yeah."

"You don't know what wield means?"

"No," he said, as he stood there wielding.

"Public school, right?" I said.

"I want my cat back!" Tirzah said.

"It's *my* cat!" Bat Boy said.

"You two can settle this later," I said, taking a step toward Bat Boy.

He wielded even more.

"Put the bat down now," I said. "Or I'm going to take it from you and use it to give you a colonoscopy."

"A what?" he said.

"Just drop the bat."

He shook his head.

I took another step. We were about five feet apart.

Every major league hitter has to begin his swing with a slight hitch of the bat as he begins his forward step. It's unavoidable. It takes a fraction of a second. Which is all I needed.

I began with a good old karate *kiai*, the energy scream exploding out from the *transversus abdominis*, and which momentarily freezes the nerves of an opponent.

Bat Boy's hands jerked downward, like an eye blink, no force in it. By the time he started to raise the bat again my right foot hammered his chest. The force drove him backward, into the driver's side door of his truck. His body slamming made a sound like a Salvation Army drum.

Both his hands dropped.

I moved in and gave him a right elbow to the cheekbone.

As he fell I grabbed the bat. File this under Baby, Candy From.

"You killed him!" Tirzah said.

She rushed at me, throwing punches. They landed like pillows.

I pushed her away.

"Are you kidding me?" I said.

She cursed at me, then dropped to her knees to look after Bat Boy.

He was out.

"What about your cat?" I said.

"Leave us alone!"

This was my witness.

I threw the bat so it whirligigged upward and onto the roof of the apartment building.

Then I got in Spinoza and left.

"Our client is lying to us," I said.

"I'm shocked, shocked," Ira said.

"He was not with Tirzah Horrick."

"You know this how?"

"She cracked like a robin's egg."

It was mid-afternoon and we were in Ira's living room office. Once more he offered me tea, and once more I told him to keep his dried leaves to himself.

A bit snappishly, which prompted him to say, "What happened, Michael?"

"Happened?"

"You have that look about you."

"Look?"

"Can't you answer me without a question?"

"Question?"

"Hopeless," Ira said.

"Don't give up on me," I said.

"Let's think," Ira said.

"Always a good idea."

"Our client could be protecting someone. Or does not want to reveal his real alibi. He tried to get this poor girl to lie for him, and she's apparently not doing a good job. Anything else you get from her?"

"Not really," I said. "I did talk to her boyfriend."

"What did he have to say?"

"Not much. He tried to steal her cat and threatened to use my head as a baseball."

"Don't tell me."

"Here we go again," I said.

"How bad is he?" Ira said.

"I just put him to sleep. But you'll be happy to know it was a Krav Maga elbow strike that did it."

"I'm thrilled."

"I did that one for you."

"I'm honored Michael, but can you at least try to go a week without beating somebody up?"

"If people would just play nice," I said.

"You know, you can always retreat."

"I am not familiar with that word," I said.

"And yet you're always on the run."

"How's that?"

"I don't have to tell you. You know."

"I'm not in the mood for riddles."

"When it comes to you, you never are," Ira said.

"Oh boy," I said. "Here comes another wise, soul-searching lecture from the rabbi."

What I couldn't stand then was the look in Ira's eyes. Subtle but clear. He was hurt. It's what I do to everyone eventually.

"Look," I said, "what do we do about Archie? Want me to go down to the jail and chew his ear off?"

"Why don't I put you to good use instead?"

"I have a good use?"

"Like a burro with a solid bit," Ira said. "After all, if God used Balaam's ass, he can certainly use you. What's troubling about this case?"

"Besides everything? Let me think ..."

"Motive," Ira said. "We can argue lack of motive. In a case of circumstantial evidence, that's something for the jury to consider."

I said, "But the prosecution doesn't have to prove motive."

"Right. But without one, their case weakens. For that I give you the case of People v. Vereneseneckockockhoff."

"Quit kidding around," I said.

"That's a real case, out of the Supreme Court of California, in 1899. And it has never been vacated or overruled. It says that while motive is not the ultimate fact to be proven, the proof *or disproof* of any motive or inducement to commit the crime is an important consideration, *especially* in a case depending upon circumstantial evidence."

"Man, 1899? Vecker snecker hoff?"

"Vereneseneckockockhoff," Ira said. "And I just want a chance to throw that out to the judge."

"That still leaves us with a lying client," I said.

"He can be convinced."

"A good, swift kick in the groin, I'm thinking."

"Coercion is not persuasion," Ira said.

"Doesn't the Bible say a little coercion goes a long way?"

"What translation are you quoting?"

"The Chuck Norris Standard Version," I said.

"Don't bring it to court," Ira said. "See you tomorrow morning for Mr. Jennison's arraignment."

B efore heading back to the beach I walked a block to where my friend Henry lived. Henry is ten, and had been picked on by a bully at school. The school refused to do anything about it. With his mother's permission I taught Henry a couple of self-defense moves.

I knocked on the door and Henry's mother answered. Teresa Martinez is in her early thirties, a single mom working out of her home as an accountant.

"Mike! Come in."

We went to the living room where she offered me some coffee. I deferred, saying I just wanted to check and see how Henry was doing with the school situation.

"You need to sit down," she said. Teresa has brown eyes that seem interested in everything and flash with intensity when Henry is the subject.

I sat. Teresa paced.

"He was confronted by that bully," Teresa said. "Henry was wearing a new jacket and that boy had greasy hands from eating something, chicken I think, and he wiped his hands on Henry's jacket. Henry told him to cut it out and the boy pushed him and said, 'Make me.' So Henry made him."

The way she said it made me smile.

"He got him on the ground, the way you showed him, and in a ..." She made a gesture, her hand grabbing her opposite wrist.

"*Hadaka jime*," I said. "Judo chokehold."

"Yes! And he did it like you said, just to control, not to harm."

"That's good to hear."

"Not according to the school!" Her eyes were on fire. "They took Henry out of the class and now they're making him see a counselor."

"Have you objected to this?"

"I was told it was mandatory or Henry would not be allowed back in school."

"But did you have a meeting with the principal?"

"I tried to set one up but he said the matter was closed."

I shook my head. "It's a public school, not a stalag. Can we hop on your laptop?"

She had it open on the dining room table. I searched for *California public school parental rights* and at the top of the results was the California Education Code, section 51101.

I went to the page and started to read. "Parents and guardians of pupils enrolled in public schools have the right and should have the opportunity, as mutually supportive and respectful partners in the education of their children within the public schools, to be informed by the school, and to participate in the education of their children."

"What a concept," Teresa said.

"Says you have the right to request to meet with the child's teacher and the principal, and it should be granted within a reasonable time. Why don't you type out that request and make a reference to the code section?"

"That's a great idea."

"Then give it to me and I'll hand deliver it. It would be easy to ignore if it came through the mail."

"You don't have to get involved in this, Mike."

"I figure I'm already involved," I said.

A woman at the front desk stood up to greet me at the counter.

"I'd like to see the principal, if I may," I said.

"Do you have an appointment?" the woman said. She was pleasant about it. Considering who I'd been running around with, pleasant was good.

"I don't, but I wanted to hand deliver this." I held up the envelope.

She looked at it as if it might contain something nasty or poisonous.

"It's a request to meet," I said. "From the parent of one of your students, Henry Martinez."

"Oh yes," she said, with hesitation.

"It beats the mail," I said. "And this way I know the principal will receive it."

"He's not in at the moment," the woman said. "If you'd like to leave it with me ..."

She looked up then as a thin gent in a charcoal suit came in behind me.

"Dr. Crosland," she said. "This man has something for you."

Crosland looked at me with a forced smile, a price paid by admins who have to deal with the public.

"It's from Teresa Martinez."

That got his attention.

"Will you step into my office, please?" he said.

"Be glad to."

His office was pristine. It looked like dust would take one look and run away in fear. He closed the door and asked me to have a seat.

I had a seat.

So did he, behind his desk.

"Are you a process server?" he said.

"Not at all," I said. "A friend of the family."

I handed him the envelope. He opened it, took out the note, read it.

"You are Mr. Romeo?" he said.

I nodded. "Mrs. Martinez wanted you to know I'm not just some guy off the street."

"May I ask what your connection is with this matter?"

"I'm the guy who taught Henry how to take down the bully."

Dr. Crosland had a pronounced Adam's apple that went up a couple of floors and back down again.

"I can't say I approve of that," he said.

"Why not?" I said.

"We just can't allow violence on our campus, Mr. Romeo."

"It's not a question of allowing, is it?"

"What do you mean?"

"I mean, it happens anyway. Boys will be boys, as they say. At least, they used to. I guess you can't say it anymore. But it's true nonetheless. There will always be bullies."

"We certainly do our best in that regard."

"Do you?"

He snapped a look at me.

"I imagine you're stuck with whatever the policy is around here," I said.

"The policy is a good one."

"Has bullying gone down?"

He snapped another look.

"I'm not here to throw stones," I said. "Everybody knows bullying's a problem that's getting worse. Heck, society's getting worse. Why should we think schools are immune?"

"You talk like someone with a degree in something."

"I'd rather have common sense," I said. "College degrees seem to suck that out these days."

I looked at Dr. Crosland's doctoral degree, framed, hanging on the wall. He noticed my look.

I said, "I'll let Mrs. Martinez discuss this with you further."

"Wait," he said. "I'd like to hear what you have to say."

"Off the record?" I said.

"Sure," he said.

"I don't want any of this held against Henry," I said.

"I assure you it won't be."

"All right," I said. "You can't equate the bully and the defender.

By putting both Henry and this other kid in counseling, you send that message. Any boy or girl has the absolute right to defend themselves in a situation where there is no other alternative."

"We encourage any student who is being bullied to talk to a caring adult, and avoid places where they might come into contact with the bully."

"But sometimes there isn't going to be a choice, right?"

"Unfortunately."

"And you can't put all the burden on the kid getting bullied," I said. "He has a right to walk the campus just like any other kid. And if the bully pushes the limit, the kid has a right to defend himself."

"The rights of the students are given by policy," Dr. Crosland said.

"There are rights that transcend anyone's policy," I said.

"I'm not sure I agree," he said.

"Then maybe you should take that down." I pointed to a framed Declaration of Independence on his wall.

He looked at it. So did his Adam's apple.

He tapped the desk with the note.

"Dr. Crosland," I said, "I know you've got a tough job. You've got charge over kids. What happens here will stay with them, maybe the rest of their lives. All Mrs. Martinez is asking is to be heard and for her son to feel like he can take care of himself if he has no other choice."

At least he thought about it before answering. "Of course I will meet with her," he said. Then added, "I can't promise anything will be done differently."

"Isn't that the definition of insanity?" I said.

"Excuse me?"

"Doing the same things over and over and expecting different results. But I've said enough." I stood. "I usually do."

. . .

A rchie's arraignment was on Thursday morning at the Airport Courthouse, where the snarl of the 405 and the snarl of the 105 meet and snarl together. It took me twenty minutes to get into the parking structure and up to the courtroom where Archie was going to make his first appearance before a magistrate.

Ira was sitting in the first row of the courtroom chatting with another attorney. I took a seat next to Ira. He introduced me to the lawyer, a prosperous-looking man in a suit who shook my hand and said, "Ira's told me a lot about you."

"Loose lips sink ships," I said.

"And lose criminal cases," the lawyer said.

"I'm sandwiched by wisdom," Ira said.

I took a quick look around the courtroom. A bunch of people sat there, waiting for their lawyers to show up, or to support a family member being formally charged. It looked like an equal mix of black, Latino, and white. An old guy sat in the far corner. Silver-haired with a black eye patch over his left orb. Dressed in a sharp suit. He could have stepped out of a scotch ad from a 1965 Life magazine.

You get all kinds in court.

Through a side door, a sheriff's deputy marched in three holds. Archie was one of them. He looked dazed and lost. The deputy directed the three men, whose hands were shackled to leather belts, to sit in the jury box.

Ira got up, using his forearm crutches, and had me follow him to the box. The bailiff kept an eye on us as Archie leaned over the rail.

"Did you talk to Tirzah?" he asked.

"Michael did," Ira said.

"And?"

"Archie," I said, "she won't hold up. You weren't with her."

"No way! I was!"

Ira said, "If you lie to us, Mr. Jennison, we can't be any help to you."

He looked at us, back and forth.

"I didn't do it," he said.

"Why'd you set up a phony alibi?" I said.

He didn't answer.

"Mr. Jennison," Ira said, "you are facing a second-degree murder charge. That's fifteen-to-life. Don't play games."

"This isn't a game," Archie said. "Just call it off."

"Call what off?" Ira said.

"I don't want your help anymore," Archie said.

Ira put his hand on my arm, a reflexive move, I'm sure. He thought I might slap Archie right then and there. And he was right.

Ira said, "Why would you say that?"

"I'm tired," Archie said.

"No you're not," I said. "What are you afraid of?"

"Just let it go," Archie said.

"Where were you Tuesday night?" I said.

"Let it go!" Archie said.

That's when the judge came out and took the bench.

The bailiff told Archie to sit down. That was our cue to go back to the row of chairs just inside the bar to wait for our case to be called.

"This is going to be dicey," Ira whispered to me after we were seated.

"Ya think?" I said.

The bailiff, who had moved to his desk on the side of the courtroom near where we were seated, cleared his throat and shot me a be-quiet look.

I get that a lot.

There were two arraignments before ours. A robbery and an assault and battery. It sounded like a game of Can You Top This? We were about to top them both.

. . .

Judge Richard Acker called the case of People v. Jennison. The Deputy DA, a fresh-faced Ivy Leaguer named Kent Hayhurst, stood. I can tell Ivy Leaguers ten feet away. I had been one once. He had the clean-cut air of someone born to privilege and using the DA's office as a stepping stone for a political career. He would knife someone in the back, figuratively speaking, to get to the head of the office someday.

"Ready for the People," Kent Hayhurst said.

Ira stood. "Good morning, Your Honor. Ira Rosen on behalf of Mr. Jennison. We will waive a reading of the complaint and a statement of rights, and enter a plea of not guilty."

"Hey!" Archie said, shooting to his feet.

Judge Acker glared at Archie. "Sir, you will not speak unless I say you can speak."

"I got rights!"

"Your Honor," Ira said quickly, "my client needs some time to talk this over with me."

The judge still had his eyes on Archie. "Is Mr. Rosen your lawyer?"

"No."

"Sit down and be quiet," Judge Acker said.

Ira said, "Your Honor—"

Archie shouted, "He's fired. I represent myself."

"No, you do not, Mr. Jennison," Judge Acker said. "One more word and you go back to lockup."

"This is unconstitutional!" Archie said.

"Get him out of here," the judge said to the bailiff at the desk. There was another, beefier bailiff near the jury box. The two of them marched Archie through the back door of the courtroom.

I looked behind me at the gallery and saw more than a few smiles at the entertainment. The guy with the patch was not smiling.

"I hope he's already paid you, Mr. Rosen," the judge said. That elicited several laughs in the courtroom.

"All is not butter that comes from a cow," Ira said.

"He is still your cow," Judge Acker said. "I'm entering a plea of not guilty and setting this for a competency hearing on the matter of representation. What about bail?"

"People obviously request remand, Your Honor," Hayhurst said.

That was fine with us. But even though jail was the best place for Archie at the moment, Ira was bound to represent the interest of his client. Ethics. They exist for many reasons, and Ira knows them all.

"On the matter of bail, Your Honor," Ira said. "Mr. Jennison has no prior record and there is no likelihood that his release would endanger anyone."

Kent Hayhurst said, "I believe Mr. Jennison has been a martial arts fighter, and did at one time attend a court-ordered anger management program."

"That was eight years ago," Ira said. "And no charges were filed against Mr. Jennison."

Hayhurst, looking at the file, said, "It was an arrest for domestic violence."

"Who was the alleged victim?" Judge Acker asked. "Same as the deceased?"

"No, Your Honor," Ira said. "The woman in that matter withdrew her complaint."

"We all know how that goes," Hayhurst said.

The judge nodded. "Bail is set at one million," he said.

W e went back to talk to Archie in lockup.

"I'll handle this, Ira," I said. "I know how to talk to him."

"Go ahead," Ira said.

"You stupid jerk!" I said to Archie. "What are you trying to pull?"

"Terrific," Ira said.

"Just let me alone," Archie said.

"What is going on in that melon of yours?" I said.

"Nothing!"

"I believe that," I said. "Which means you're not thinking straight. You're not thinking at all."

"You're both fired," he said.

"Not until the judge says we are," I said.

"What!"

"There has to be a competency hearing," Ira said.

"No way!" Archie said. "Just leave me alone, okay?"

"We can't do that, Arch," I said. "We represent you. You're stuck with us at least until the hearing."

"That's insane!" Archie said. "This is America!"

"And in America," I said, "we take care of the insane."

"I'm not talking anymore," Archie said. "So don't bother coming back."

O utside the courthouse the day was looking gloomy. The west side marine layer was light gray and misty.

"What exactly is our obligation now?" I said.

"We are to represent him zealously," Ira said. "Until we're told he can cut us loose."

"So why don't I find out the truth?" I said. "That's always a good thing, isn't it?"

"According to your arm," Ira said.

L ater, I called Zane Donahue's number. Got a man's voice—at least, I think it was a man, but these days steroidal manipulation may play some havoc with that clue. I told the voice that it was Mike Romeo and that I'd like to meet with Donahue for about fifteen minutes. I was told to hold on.

I held on.

A couple of minutes went by. There wasn't even any hold

music. I felt cheated. I started singing the Jets song from *West Side Story*. When I got to "Little boy, you're a man..." the voice came back on.

"Mr. Donahue will meet you, at a time and place of his choosing. Agreeable?"

"He's the top cat in town," I said.

"Excuse me?"

"The gold medal kid. Which means yes, agreeable. When and where?"

"Two hours. At Jimmy's, in the Valley."

"Done," I said. "But no zip guns or chains."

"What are you talking about?"

"I'm just amusing myself. I'll be there."

"If it was up to me, I'd tell Mr. Donahue to ignore your sorry—"

I hung up.

"My man!"

Jimmy Sarducci greeted me the moment I walked through the door of his boxing and MMA facility. Jimmy is five-four in heeled shoes. He was once a Golden Gloves champ in the flyweight division. Came up in the tough gyms of East Los Angeles. Now he trains fighters and does consulting work in Hollywood. The only reason Stallone looks like he knows what he's doing in a ring is because of Jimmy.

"Who's your next champ, Jimmy?" I said, shaking his hand.

"You are, Mike. When you coming on board?"

"I'm not a fighter, Jimmy. I'm into poetry now."

"Aw, don't kid a kidder." Jimmy has a staccato way of speaking, in keeping with his Italian bloodline.

"I just want people to love each other," I said.

"Yeah, right," Jimmy said. "Nothin' says love like a good right cross."

"You're a true romantic."

"You working out today?"

I shook my head. "Meeting Zane Donahue."

"Zane's coming by?"

I nodded.

"That's big stuff," Jimmy said. "He don't come by lest it's something important."

"I'm important," I said.

"You're a tomato can. But if I train you ..."

"Don't kid a kidder," I said.

Jimmy left me for a word with some pug, so I wandered over to the ring to watch a couple of black fighters sparring. One of them looked good. A middleweight, I guessed. He had great abs and even better footwork. The other one wasn't so agile. He was a little bigger, but that old cliché came to mind—the harder they fall.

Zane Donahue walked in with a woman. A formidable woman. An enhanced woman. A fighting woman. She had long blonde hair in a severe ponytail that looked like it would pull back if you tried to pull it first. Eyes the blue of a blowtorch. They were sure burning a hole in me.

"Hello, Mike," Zane Donahue said. "I'd like you to meet somebody. This is Malita Faust."

The blues eyes glowed hotter. I put out my hand. She ignored it. Her entire left arm was decked out in colorful tattoos. I could make out a horse and chariot and what looked like Roman soldiers.

"She's one of my up and comers," Donahue said.

"Friendly sort," I said.

"You want to try me?" Malita Faust said. She was already dressed in black spandex. All she needed was some gloves. Or maybe not even those.

"Now, now," Donahue said. "This is not the way to start things out."

"What are we starting?" I said.

Zane Donahue turned to Malita Faust. "Why don't you go start a workout, and I'll get with you in a few."

She gave me one more blue flame before walking away.

"Sweet girl," I said.

"She's good. Another Rousey. I'm bringing her along slow."

"She doesn't look slow to me," I said.

"You wanted to talk to me about Archie Jennison," Donahue said.

"How'd you know that?" I said.

"Mike, information is the coin of my realm. I know all about Archie and you and that rabbi lawyer. I know Archie's trying to convict himself."

A picture flashed into my mind. "The guy with the eye patch," I said.

Donahue eyed me, silent.

"In court," I said. "There was a well-dressed gent sitting in the corner. Had a pirate eye patch. He works for you, doesn't he?"

Zane Donahue smiled. "You are very good, Mike. We could make a great team."

"You don't have to spy on me," I said.

"No spying, Mike. I look after my assets, that's all."

"I'm not your asset," I said.

"I'm talking about Archie," Donahue said. "I can wait for you."

"Then you know why I wanted to talk to you."

"You want to know how you can find out if Archie really did it."

"I don't think he did," I said.

"You know he's capable of it."

"I think he's scared."

"What do you think he's scared of?"

"No idea. I thought maybe you could tell me."

"How well do you know Archie?" Donahue said.

"I knew him about twelve years ago. He was kind of a loose cannon then."

"He hasn't changed. That's what makes him a good fighter. Or did. He's starting to slip."

"What's he into?" I said.

"Meaning?"

"PEDs?"

Donahue paused. "You think Archie's on something?"

"Don't you know?"

"There are certain questions I don't care to ask," Donahue said. "What a guy takes, who he sleeps with."

"He's probably using, and it's probably affecting his mind."

"Might that make him capable of killing somebody?"

"It might," I said. "But I don't think he did."

"I don't either," Donahue said. "That's why I brought Malita."

"Oh?"

"She can help you. She knows more about Archie than anybody. She can tell you who his friends are, who you should talk to."

I looked over at Malita Faust, who was kicking the heavy bag and giving a little scream each time.

"Is it safe to talk to her without a stun gun?" I said.

He laughed. "She's a sweetheart once you get to ..."

Donahue stopped talking, looked over my shoulder. "But I'm not so sure about this one."

I turned.

Die Scum was walking toward us.

All warfare, wrote Sun Tzu, is based on deception. Hence, when able to attack, we must seem unable. When using our forces, we must seem inactive. When we are near, we must make the enemy believe we are far. When far, we must make him believe we are near. We feign disorder in order to crush him.

And at all times be ready to kick a guy in the nerts. Sun Tzu never said that, but he should have.

"Chicken Heart's here," Die Scum said. He was in a tight black T-shirt and black sweatpants. His black heart was concealed, but betrayed by his bad breath and flurry of trash talk, which he gave me nose-to-nose. "You ready to do this thing or not, woman? Your boyfriend not want you to fight anymore?"

"Hamburger with onions?" I said.

"What?"

"Your lunch," I said. "I'm guessing Carl's Jr."

Zane Donahue said, "Now hold on, Casey. This isn't the time or place."

"Never will be, with this guy," Die Scum said. Try as I might, I couldn't think of him as a Casey. Or any other normal name.

"He's gutless," Die Scum said.

"I've stored my guts in the freezer," I said.

He pushed in, almost touching my nose now. Onions, burger *and* mustard.

"Bite me," Die Scum said.

"Break it up, guys," Zane Donahue said.

"What's wrong with right now?" Die Scum said. "There's the ring."

"I just washed my hair," I said.

Mr. Scum then did a very ungentlemanly thing. He pushed me, the same way I pushed him into the pool at Donahue's house.

I stumbled back, slipped, went down on my arse.

As the whole gym stopped and looked.

I got to my feet, smoothed out my shirt. It had pineapples and surfers on it.

Die Scum readied his fists.

Zane Donahue stood silent.

"Nice try," I said to Donahue.

And walked on by, just like Dionne Warwick would have wanted me to.

I could almost feel the confusion between Scum and Donahue. Zane had set the whole thing up. Wanted to bait me. But I wasn't going to be his anchovy.

Malita Faust had one hand on the heavy bag, watching me as I approached.

"We need to talk," I said.

W e walked outside, onto Victory Boulevard, and set off in the general direction of Tommy's Hamburgers on Topanga.

"Why didn't you take him on?" Malita said. She walked as if she were challenging the sidewalk to a fight.

"I'm not a dancing monkey," I said.

"What does that even mean?"

"You always do what Zane Donahue tells you to do?"

"No way."

"Name me one time you didn't," I said.

She thought about it. Then cursed.

"You're a dancing monkey," I said.

"I don't have to take that from you," she said.

"Zane told you to talk to me, right?" I said.

She cursed again.

"I'll buy you a hamburger," I said. "You like chili-cheese fries?"

T ommy's is the home of the best burger and chili-cheese fries in the city. A gastric Mecca for day laborers, IT workers, and the occasional hipster. As I held the door for her I said, "Whoever did your ink did a nice job."

She held out her arm. "You like?"

I took her wrist and rotated the arm a little. "You've got Roman soldiers in a battle against a woman on a chariot, holding a spear."

"Know who that is?"

"Wouldn't be Queen Boudica, would it?"

Her mouth fell open. "You are the first person ever to know that."

"What do I win?"

There were a few people in the ordering line ahead of us.

Malita did not seem to notice. She was turned completely toward me.

She said, "I mean it. How did you know ?"

"I used to read cereal boxes as a kid," I said.

"Come on!"

"I read Tacitus and Roman history."

"You some sort of brainiac?"

"No way. I was born right here in this country."

She frowned. Then got it. Then punched my shoulder.

"So what's that writing on your arm?" she said.

"It's a Latin phrase. It means truth conquers all things."

"So you always tell the truth?"

"I always seek it. Most of the time I try to speak it, too."

"Most of the time?"

I said, "When someone would use the truth to hurt someone else, I'd withhold it."

"Like when?" she said.

"Oh, like if someone was going to use it to kill somebody else. My friend and sometime employer, a rabbi, likes to tell the story of the Hebrew midwives in the book of Exodus. Are you familiar with that story?"

She shook her head.

"Well, Pharaoh didn't want the Israelite slaves to continue breeding. So he ordered the midwives to kill any Hebrew baby boys by drowning them."

"That's terrible!"

"But these two midwives feared God and didn't do what Pharaoh said. They kept saving the Hebrew boys. Pharaoh found out about it, and brought them in and said, what the heck are you doing? I told you to kill them. So the two midwives told him a fib. They said that the Hebrew women were more vigorous than the Egyptian women, so the babies always came out before they got there."

"And this Pharaoh guy bought that?"

"He was a couple of bricks short of a pyramid. The point is, though, that the Bible says God dealt kindly with these midwives. Their deception was for a greater good."

"Man, you are a thinker, aren't you?" she said.

"Order up," I said.

She looked at the order options posted by the window.

"You really eat this stuff?" she said.

"Lunch of Champions."

"You're crazy."

"What'll you have?"

"Nothing."

"You're skin and bones."

For that she gave me another punch in the shoulder.

"That feel like skin and bones?" she said.

I rubbed my shoulder. "You'll have some chili-cheese fries. And like them."

When I got to the window I ordered a Tommy Burger, chili-cheese fries and a Coke.

"I don't want anything," Malita said.

"Eve said the same thing in the garden," I said. "Prepare to be tempted."

When we sat down with the food, I put the chili-cheese fries between us and handed Malita a plastic fork.

"You'll thank me," I said.

"Just so you'll shut up about it." She took the fork and stabbed a fry. Looked at it for a second, popped it in her mouth.

Without a change in her expression, she chomped.

I knew she was going to crack.

"Okay," she said. "That was good."

"Let's share," I said. "While you tell me about Archie. You don't think he killed his girlfriend, do you?"

She shook her head, stabbed another fry.

I said, "Archie doesn't have an alibi for the time of the murder. He made one up and tried to get someone to lie for him—"

"Tirzah Horrick," she said, and then jammed the fry in her mouth.

"Not a fan?"

"She's worthless. A druggie."

"What's her connection to Archie?"

"She hung around with him for awhile. Then he took up with Missy, and that was that, except for a couple of scenes."

"Scenes?"

"Screaming and crying. Girl stuff. Makes me sick. You know, these really are delicious." She stabbed more fries.

"Do you have any idea where Archie might have been on Tuesday?"

"No."

"Anybody he should be scared of?"

She looked at me. "There's always people hanging around our game."

"Like the guy with the eye patch?"

That brought her up short. "What do you know about him?"

"Nothing," I said. "It's why I'm asking you."

"I don't like him," Malita said. "Has a lot of money, I think. Tight with Zane."

"Why don't you like him?"

She shrugged. "Some people rub me the wrong way."

"Like me?"

Smile. "I'm warming up to you, big boy."

"And all I had to do was ply you with some chili-cheese fries."

"I'm an easy date," she said. "When do you want to go out?"

"I'm sorry?"

"Out. You. Me. A date."

I cleared my throat. "Maybe we should keep it strictly business for now."

"Not gonna happen," she said.

"At least pump the brakes. This is about Archie."

"Okay," she said. "Archie. What else do you want to know?"

Before I could answer the doors of Tommy's flew open and a

big guy stormed in, followed by a petite woman. They were both Hispanic, late twenties. The guy's face was screwed up in anger. The woman's face was screwed up in worry.

Modern romance.

I said, "Any idea about who might have wanted Missy dead?"

She didn't answer right away, but I could tell her gears were churning. Then she nodded.

"Guy she was involved with before Archie," she said. "Name's Rory. Rory O'Connor."

"The luck of the Irish," I said.

"Guy's not lucky," she said. "He's bad news. Used to hit her. Made threats when she took up with Archie."

"You know this how?"

"It was at a party. Got ugly."

"Anybody else—" I stopped because the big guy at the order window told the woman to shut up. Loud enough for everybody in the place to hear.

"Now that's just rude," Malita said.

I said, "Anybody else you know might have something against Missy?"

She shook her head.

"What else can you tell me about this O'Connor?" I said.

"Stay away from him," she said.

"Maybe I can go around him."

"How?"

"Does he have a girlfriend?"

She thought a moment. "Ex. Her name's Derinda Tyman."

"Know where I can find her?"

"Sure," she said. "She works at the Walmart over on Fallbrook."

"So do a lot of people."

"You'll recognize her. She's tall and has hot pink hair. You can ask somebody."

I paused to dig into my Tommy burger, and watch Malita's eyes dance a little as she ate more fries.

The silence was broken by voices. The big guy and his woman

were arguing by the napkin dispenser. He was jamming his finger at her. More of that and I was going to have to get up.

Then Malita said, "Hey! People are trying to eat here."

This got the big guy's attention. He turned his head, then his body. Then started for our table.

"You got somethin' to say?" he said to Malita.

I made a move to slide out from our table but Malita put her arm on mine.

"I got this," she said.

And stood up.

L ife has moments to savor.

There's the first time you taste an ice cream sundae as a kid, with your mom and dad and it's delivered to the table with all the whipped cream and a cherry on top.

Sometimes, such moments sneak up on you, take you by surprise. But once they start happening, you just sit back and enjoy. Like baby's first step or the first time they say *Mama*.

Could be in sports. Did you see Kirk Gibson's home run in the 1988 World Series? Or Curt Schilling's bloody sock pitching classic against the Yankees?

Or it just might be in a fast food joint when an MMA-trained woman stands up to an overweight blowhard who has no idea what's coming.

The big guy asked Malita if she wanted to say something else, and ended his inquiry by calling her that name which begins with the second letter of our alphabet.

Malita delivered one of the best and fastest side-snap kicks I've ever seen. To the guy's chin. Her extension was amazing.

The guy's head snapped back like a Pez dispenser.

Using the power of her hips, Malita followed with a full-thrust kick to the heart. That knocked him into a trash receptacle. He bounced off it and as he did Malita performed a technically precise spin kick that caught him full on the right side of his face.

The hulk went down like the Hindenburg, but not before his face hit the edge of an empty table.

Oh, the humanity.

The whole thing took four seconds.

The woman stood frozen at the order counter, her hands over her mouth.

"You okay?" Malita said to her.

The woman, eyes wide, kept her hands on her mouth.

"You don't need to be with this guy," Malita said. "Can you get away from him?"

The woman just stared.

"You live with him?" Malita said.

The woman shook her head.

"You need help? Is there someplace you can go? Family?"

The Hindenburg was not moving. Blood flowed out of a gash on his forehead.

A man in a white shirt came out of a side door. He had manager written all over him. He looked at Malita, at the guy on the floor, then at me. It must have been my open, honest face that had him ask me, "What happened?"

I stood and motioned to the man on the floor. "This fellow was causing trouble. Your person taking orders there will testify to that. He was loud and insulting to the woman who came in with him. My companion"—I nodded toward Malita—"asked the gentleman to show some consideration. He approached our table with aggression. In self-defense, my companion removed his aggression. As he fell to the floor, he tried to damage one of your tables with his head. Your table won."

The owner was frowning at me, as if he didn't follow. I get that a lot.

Malita cracked up.

The poor female victim didn't know what to do.

"I am calling police," the owner said.

"Tell them to bring an ambulance," I said.

. . .

I t took an hour to straighten things out. Two patrol officers, a man and a woman, took our statements, a statement from the woman, and a couple from people who'd been witnesses to the whole thing. In the end no arrests were made. A paramedic patched up the big guy's head. He was allowed to leave with his girlfriend.

Just before the police officers left, the male officer leaned close to Malita and, with a smile, said, "Awesome."

We walked back to Jimmy's. At the door I said good-bye and thanks for the memory.

"This isn't over between us," she said.

I wasn't about to argue with her.

I gave Ira a call from Spinoza as I headed over to check out Archie's place.

"I need you to run a name," I said. "Rory O'Connor. He was Missy's boyfriend before Archie. Got physical with her. I also got the name of his current girlfriend from a source. Her name is Derinda Tyman."

"So who was this source?" Ira said.

"She's a little offbeat," I said.

"She?"

"Uh-huh."

"Offbeat how?" Ira said.

"Well, I guess you could say she can beat up most men."

"What a fine quality to have," Ira said.

"I kind of like it," I said.

"Michael, is this—"

"It's nothing, just a source." Or so I was telling myself. "I'm going over to Archie's building and do a little canvassing. I'll take a look at his apartment. Anything else you want me to do?"

"Moderate your behavior," Ira said.

"I'll think about it," I said.

. . .

Archie Jennison lived in an apartment in Venice. You needed some good scratch to live there. Arch had to be doing pretty well for himself. The apartment was in his name and he'd lived there for three years.

The building was a three-story job the color of a dead elephant's tusk. Two fake doors were painted on the front wall. One blue, one green, complete with painted-on doorknobs. Fake doors to nowhere. Sometimes symbolism kicks you right in the face.

Between them was a real door. Using one of Archie's keys, I unlocked it. Archie's apartment was on the second floor. I took the stairs to get there. The corridor was as colorless as the outside. Hip-hop blasted from one of the apartments and echoed down the hall.

I let myself into Archie's and closed the door.

There was a TV on one wall, with floor speakers on either side of it. On a table next to the right speaker was a fishbowl.

A black faux-leather sofa faced the TV, with a coffee table in front of it. There were three magazines on the floor. They were men's muscle mags—*Flex, Iron Man, Men's Health*—the kind that show juicers flexing their guns and are stuffed with ads for supplements and aminos.

Everything looked pretty normal, which meant the crime scene team didn't spend a whole lot of time tossing the place. That was because Missy Nolan had been found dead on the sofa, asphyxiated. One of the cushions was apparently used to snuff the life out of her.

There was no blood. No fingerprints. Nothing biological taken for DNA testing. No sexual violation. Missy had been fully clothed. Whoever did the killing did it neat and clean.

Nor was there breaking and entering.

Which was one big circumstantial evidence mark next to Archie's name.

I looked around a little without finding anything of interest, except in the goldfish bowl. On top of the cloudy water floated a dead fish.

As I wondered whether I should dump the water and give the fish a proper burial in the toilet, a voice behind me said, "Who are you?"

I t was a woman in her mid-forties. She was thin, almost frail. She wore black pants and a black-with-white-stripes blouse that look faded. She had pronounced worry lines in her forehead. Her eyes were brown, but rimmed with red. She'd been drinking or crying, or both.

"My name's Mike Romeo," I said.

"What are you doing here?" she said.

"I'm on business."

"What business?"

"Legal."

She gave me a study. She had a purse hanging from one of her skinny arms. For a second I thought she might try to hit me with it.

"Are you working for him?" she said.

"Who?" I said.

"The scumbag who killed my daughter."

"You're Missy's mother?"

"Just get out," she said.

"I'm sorry," I said.

"I don't care what you are. Just go."

"This is official business."

"I don't care!"

"This is Archie's apartment," I said. "I have permission to be here."

"Missy gave me a key. This was her place, too."

"Maybe we can help each other."

"Why would I help you?" she said.

"To get the real killer."

She frowned. "You're supposed to say that."

"Would it help if I told you I honestly don't think Archie is guilty?"

She shook her head.

"What if there's a chance?" I said.

"I don't care."

"If he isn't guilty, it means the real killer is still out there."

With a big sigh she started rumbling around in her purse. She pulled out a cigarette and a lighter, and lit up.

"I don't care what happens to him," she said.

I said, "We still have a presumption of innocence in this country."

"I don't care!"

"I think you care very deeply."

She cocked her head at that one, then took a long puff on her cig. "You don't seem normal to me."

"Give me a few minutes of your time," I said. "I think we might end up on the same side."

She thought about it, then shrugged and sat on the sofa. "I don't suppose there's an ashtray in this place."

"Let me see what I can do," I said. I went into the kitchen and found a porcelain saucer in a cupboard. I brought it back and put it on the coffee table.

"May I know your name?" I said.

"Kathy," she said.

I sat in the chair next to the sofa.

"I really don't think I should talk to you," she said. "Anything I say you can use against me."

"You're not accused of anything, Kathy."

"I mean, to help that jerk."

"Can you at least tell me why you think that?"

She shrugged. "I suppose that can't hurt."

I waited. She took another drag and flicked some ashes into the saucer.

"He was just using her for sex," she said. "But he kept saying he loved her."

"Maybe he did."

"I know the type. Big charmer. Say anything to anybody. He's twenty years older than Missy. What he did to her."

"What was it?" I asked.

"She started going downhill when she moved in with him. It was drugs. We had a fight about it once, and she kept telling me I was wrong. All I know is she was once just full of life and her skin was good and she was in great shape. And then she wasn't. The only thing that could have caused that was the man she got mixed up with."

"Could she have been sick?" I said.

"She would have told me," Kathy said.

"Were you on speaking terms?"

Silence. Then: "Do you have children, Mr. ..."

"Romeo."

"Is that your real name?"

"Yes."

"Well, do you?"

"No."

"Think long and hard before you have any," she said. "It's the hardest thing in the world, and then they end up dead."

She stubbed out her cigarette and folded her arms, as if to keep warm.

"She was all I had," Kathy said. "Her father wanted nothing to do with her. I was eighteen and he was twenty-seven and he took off for the Himalyas or India or some island. So I worked three jobs and did my best, you know? Soccer practice, cheerleader practice, swimming. She wanted to be an Olympic swimmer for a couple of years, so I got up at four o'clock and took her to the pool so she could work out before school and ... "

She was crying softly now, rocking back and forth on the sofa.

"I'm sorry," she managed to say. "Stupid."

"Not stupid at all," I said.

For a long moment we were silent. Kathy opened her purse and pulled out a Kleenex. She dabbed her eyes and under her nose.

"Can I just get her things and go?" she said.

"Sure," I said. "Just one more question. Did she ever say anything to you about a box of old photos?"

Kathy hesitated, frowned. "Photos? No."

"Nothing about Archie having some kind of newsworthy material?"

She shook her head. "Should she have?"

"Not necessarily. I just wanted to check."

"Well then," she said, and stood. "May I?"

"Of course," I said.

She headed for the bedroom and I followed. She stopped and looked at me. "You're coming?"

"If you don't mind."

"Make sure I don't steal anything?"

"I'm sure you won't. It's just part of my job."

"Your job stinks," she said.

The bedroom had been looked at by the homicide techs. The closet was open, and items that should have been on bed tables were on the bed itself. A stuffed giraffe, makeup, some clothes, a picture frame that was face down.

Kathy just stood there for a moment, staring at it all. Then she turned and went to the dresser, pulled out the top drawer. She took out a small box and laid it on top of the dresser. Opened it. She moved the items around. I heard jingling. Could have been jewelry.

"Not here," she said.

"What are you looking for?"

"Could you help me look? She had a necklace. A turquoise Indian thing, we got it on a trip to Albuquerque. She was thirteen and she fell in love with it and I bought it for her, and it was her favorite. She wore it all through high school. It clacked when she moved. It clacked ..." She had to pause. "Last time I saw her I asked about it and she said she had it in her jewelry box. It wasn't on her ... body. I'd like to have it. I'd really like ..."

That was it. The pent-up emotions of the last days caught up with her and she began crying hysterically.

This was one of those moments you don't train for. I went to her and put my hand on her shoulder. She dropped to her knees, sobbing into her hands. I got to my knees and put my arm around her shoulder. I kept it there till she cried it out.

We didn't find the necklace anywhere. I told Kathy I'd make an effort to look for it and would contact her if I did. We found a box in a closet and she filled it with several items from the bedroom. The only item of clothing she took was a powder-blue and white jacket. I saw *Missy* in white script on the front, and *Trojans Cheer* on the back. I saw the back because after Kathy folded the jacket she put it to her face, closed her eyes, and smelled it.

After she left I locked up Archie's place and started on my Joey Feint fundamentals. When I worked for this gumshoe years ago, he taught me about the boring parts first. Walking, knocking on doors, talking. Like panning for gold in a slow-moving stream, he said.

I knocked on the door across the hall. A moment later a man's voice said, "What is it?"

I said, "Can I talk to you for a minute? I'm an investigator working on the murder case."

"I already talked to the police," the voice said.

"I'm not with the police. I'm working for the accused, your neighbor, Archie Jennison."

Pause. He opened the door a crack. Through the crack I saw a plump face with a Santa Claus beard.

"You work for that slimeball?"

"Why do you say that?"

"That's what he is. Thinks he's Mr. Everything."

"That doesn't make him a murderer," I said.

"They have him in the jug, don't they?"

"That doesn't make him a murderer either."

"Good indication."

"You mind if I ask what you told the police?"

"Nothing. Didn't see or hear anything."

"Then you don't really know what happened."

"I can surmise," he said.

"That's what lynch mobs used to say."

He gave me a dose of stink eye through the door crack. "I don't know you from Adam."

"Adam wore a fig leaf. I am fully dressed. But this might help."

I took out one of Ira's lawyer cards from my shirt pocket and held it up.

"Ira Rosen is the attorney representing Mr. Jennison," I said. "I work for him. Just a couple of questions and I'll be on my way."

He opened the door a little more, took the card and looked at it, then flipped it over, then back again.

"All right," he said. "Ask."

"Out here in the hall?"

"Five minutes," he said, and opened the door.

H e was dressed in blue jeans and a white T-shirt. The jeans and shirt were spattered with paint. That was easily explained by the easel and canvas in the middle of the room, and the painting paraphernalia on a folding table next to the easel.

On a chair by one wall was a red-and-white Santa suit. My razor-sharp mind clicked.

"Department store Santa?" I said.

He snorted. "Look at me," he said. "You'd hire me for that role in a second, wouldn't you?"

"If I needed a Santa, I guess."

"I make a few bucks that way."

"Christmas has been over for weeks," I said.

"I'll get around to putting it away. Ask your questions so I can get back to work."

"Can we sit?"

"I suppose," he said. "Don't take too long." He motioned me to a chair that had a plaid shirt draped over it. He did not remove it. He pulled a folding chair from in front of the canvas, spun it to face me, and sat.

"My name's Mike," I said.

"Call me Edsel," he said.

"Like the Ford?" I said

"What else?" he said. "My dad loved that car."

"So he was the one."

"Very funny," Edsel said. "You're too young to remember the Edsel."

"I read about it."

"Bully for you. You've got four minutes left."

I said, "Do you know anything about the night of the murder?"

Edsel shook his head. "I was in Dallas, visiting a friend, Nora. She had an exhibition."

"Another painter?"

"That's right."

"How's the art world these days?" I said.

"Stinks," he said. "Commissions drying up. Galleries closing. You gotta get a lawyer for everything."

"Lawyers always win in the end."

"Ain't that the truth."

"So what was it about Archie you didn't like?" I said.

He waved his hand dismissively. "Always acting like God's gift. Walking around with his shirt off to show everybody how ripped he was. One time I told him why doesn't he put a shirt on? He says to me when I lose my gut I can talk. I wanted to take a poke at him but he's a big guy and I would've gotten my block knocked off. Things like that."

"Was he ever violent around you?"

"I tried not to have him around me."

"So you never saw him do anything destructive?"

"Just being around was destructive enough," he said.

"Did you ever hear him arguing with his girlfriend?"

He shook his head. "She I liked. She was always nice. How she ended up with him, I can't understand it."

"You know anybody else in the building you think I ought to talk to?"

Edsel almost shook his head, then said, "Won't do you any good. Chick in 3B is wacko. Never says anything to anybody. But you walk around and she pops up, like she hides in corners waiting for you. Creepy. But maybe she saw something. I don't think she goes out much. Not hard to see why."

"How's that?"

"Let's just say she's not a looker. One time I saw her in the laundry room and said hello, and she didn't say a word. She looked like a wet rat."

"That's not very gentlemanly," I said.

"It is what it is. We done here?"

I stood and circled around to take a look at the painting he was working on. To say it wasn't a Monet would be charitable. It was a painting of the Pope's head. At least I think it was supposed to be the Pope. He had that white-and-gold pope hat. The head was sticking out of a toilet.

"What do you think?" he said.

"It seems kind of odd, doesn't it?"

"What does?"

"A guy who plays Santa Claus on Christmas painting pictures that denigrate Christianity?"

"So what? You don't have to believe that jazz to play Santa and pick up a few bucks."

"You're a credit to bad Santas everywhere."

He harrumphed. "But what about the painting itself?"

"Sorry," I said.

His eyes fired up. "What do you know?"

"Art," I said.

"You don't know anything."

"I know what moral courage is. And it takes absolutely no moral courage to paint something like that."

He looked at the painting, then back at me.

"Why don't you get out of my apartment?" he said.

As I walked toward the door Bad Santa, or BS for short, shot me a string of curses.

I opened the door and looked back.

"You're going on the naughty list," I said, and closed the door behind me.

W anting a beer to wash out the taste in my mouth, I made my way to Apartment 3B, knocked, got nothing. I took the stairs to the ground floor and followed the signs to the laundry room.

There were two washers and two dryers. One of the dryers was humming. A woman matching Bad Santa's description was sitting in a chair reading a book.

She gave me a quick look. She was probably thirty but seemed older. Her eyes curved slightly downward at the corners and her short brown hair, parted in the middle, hung straight down. She wore no makeup.

And turned back to her book.

"Excuse me," I said.

It was as if I'd told her to put her hands up.

"Sorry to disturb you," I said. "My name's Mike Romeo and I'm doing some investigation about the murder that—"

"I don't know anything about it." Her head shook slightly as she spoke. She didn't make eye contact with me.

"Would you mind if I just asked one or two—"

"Please go away."

"It will only take—"

"I told you I don't know." For emphasis, she slapped the book she was reading on her lap. I saw the cover. It was *The Great Gatsby*.

"Are you enjoying it?" I said.

"Huh?"

"The book."

"Oh ... um ... sort of. I guess."

"Yeah, that was my reaction, too," I said.

"You read this?"

I think she was surprised that a guy who looked like me read something other than *Sports Illustrated*.

"Twice," I said. "Some good writing in it. Fitzgerald could craft a sentence. But the book mostly leaves me cold."

"I know!" For one second her face brightened. Then she lowered her head as if embarrassed.

I whispered like a conspirator. "We're not supposed to say such things."

In spite of herself, she smiled. Nodded.

"Who else do you like to read?" I said.

Her head came up slowly. "You're just trying to get me to talk."

I pulled a folding chair over and sat. "Is it so wrong to talk about something interesting with a stranger?"

"You want to talk about the murder."

"I do," I said. "But I really do like talking about books. Books mean a lot to me."

"Me too," she said.

"We book lovers need to stick together."

Another little smile and nod.

"May I know your name?" I said.

The smile left. "I'd rather not."

"Okay, that's fine. When I'm not reading I work for a lawyer. This lawyer is representing Archie Jennison, whose been arrested for the murder of Missy Nolan. Do you know Archie?"

"I don't talk to many people here."

"Thank you for talking to me," I said.

"I don't want to get involved," she said.

"Is there something that might involve you?"

She looked up, as if she'd let something slip out. "I just don't."

"Did the police talk to you?"

She nodded.

I said, "Was there something you didn't tell them?"

She looked at her hands.

"Would you consider telling me?" I said.

"I don't know who you are," she said. "You could be anybody."

"I'm definitely somebody," I said. "Here." I took out one of Ira's cards and handed it to her. "This is the lawyer I work for. You can call him and check me out."

"I really don't want to get involved."

"Are you afraid?"

She shook her head. Then she nodded.

"Can you tell me what you're afraid of?" I asked.

"Please don't talk to me anymore," she said.

"Maybe I can help you," I said. "I'm good at that."

She shook her head.

Some witnesses are like grapes, Joey Feint used to say. You squeeze too hard and they burst.

"Would you do me a favor then?" I said. "Would you think about it for a day, and give us a call? We're just trying to do our job in this machinery called the justice system. Would you do that for a fellow book lover?"

She took a deep breath, let it out. Then nodded.

"Thanks," I said. "I appreciate it."

I stood and started to leave.

"Hey," she said.

I turned back.

"My name is Lauren."

I took PCH back to the Cove. Traffic knotted up around the Getty Villa, but mostly it was fine. When you can move at least 25 mph in L.A. you take it and give thanks. I decided to stop at a little wine shop just past Topanga Canyon Boulevard. They were offering a tasting of their reds. I went from a zin to a cab by way of a pinot, decided I liked the cab best and ordered a glass. I took the glass to a table by the window and looked across the highway at the ocean.

The late afternoon was clear and you could see the curve of the Palos Verdes peninsula. In the middle were planes taking off from LAX, looking like little sparrows in the distance.

Which was how I felt about Archie's case. The answers were all in the distance.

There had been no reports of domestic violence between Archie and Missy Nolan. Nobody heard them argue. Except for Missy's mother and Edsel the painter, no one had anything really bad to say about Archie Jennison. Lauren the book lover didn't seem to know him well. But she did know something. I was hoping it was relevant, and that she'd give Ira a call about it.

So far we knew of no motive for Archie to kill his live-in girl-friend. Not that he didn't have one in the deep, dark recesses of his alcohol-soaked soul. Alcohol often greases the wheels of murder, but Archie didn't have any alcohol in him when he was taken in.

That was another part that was unclear. Archie had been picked up by LAPD around 9:30 a.m. at his gym. How did they know to find him there? Did somebody who knew Archie's routine tip them off? Who? And why?

And then there was the matter of Archie's clumsy alibi. When did he set that up? It had to be sometime before his arrest. Which pointed toward guilt, not innocence.

What if he had set up the alibi *before* the murder?

Now we were talking premeditation. Special circumstances. Death Row.

W hen I got back to my place I found Carter "C Dog" Weeks curled up in the chair outside my screen door.

"Hey," he said.

"What's up?" I said.

"Waitin' for you."

"Trouble?"

"Nah, no trouble." He sat up straight. "Well, yeah, trouble." He reached under the chair and dragged out a dirty duffel bag.

"The money," he said.

"Good," I said.

"You gotta make it right," C Dog said. "I'm all nervous. I can't get anything done."

I stifled a snort. "What is it that you have to do, C?"

"Write a song, things like that."

"How about getting lost in a good book?"

He shook his head.

"Why not?" I said.

"I don't read good," he said.

"Could you play a guitar the first time you picked one up?"

"No way."

"How old were you when you started?"

C Dog thought about it. "Maybe ten."

"Did somebody show you how to play?"

"Yeah. Anthony. He had a band, he was older'n me. He gave me my first lessons."

"Were you able to play *Stairway to Heaven* first time out?"

"Ha ha."

"You had to learn some basic chords, what to do with a pick, right?"

"Sure."

"And you practiced."

"Right."

"That's all reading is, and thinking, too. Practice. Come inside."

He followed me in. I tossed the duffel bag of money into the corner.

"Be careful with that," C Dog said.

"Why?" I said. "It's not yours."

He sighed, sounding like a deflating tire.

I went to the bookshelf and took out the paperback of Will Durant's *The Story of Philosophy*. "This was my first lesson in thinking. I want you to read something."

I opened to the Introduction and pointed to a line. "Read that," I said.

C Dog took the book and, slowly, read. "Most of us have known some golden days in the June of life when philosophy was in fact what Plato calls it, that dear delight."

He read *Plato* as *Platto*.

"What's that mean?" he said.

"What do you think it means?" I said.

He looked at the line again, then at me. "What does June of life mean?"

"When does June happen in any year?"

With a concentrated frown, C Dog said, "The middle?"

"Ah! So what is the June of life?"

"The middle of life?"

"Which is when you get out of adolescence. That's when you start asking bigger questions than who am I going to take to the prom, or where can I score some weed. Now, read the next part."

C Dog read, "When the love of a modestly e . . . lusive truth seemed more glorious, incomp ..."

"Incomparably."

"...comparably than the lust for the ways of the flesh and the dross of the world." He looked at me, hang dog. "Aw, man, I just don't get any of that."

"Think!"

"I'm tryin'!"

"Not hard enough," I said. "Let me ask you this. You know the feeling you get when you finally nail a difficult guitar riff? You've been trying to get the sound, and suddenly, there it is, and you think, Wow!"

"Oh, yeah!"

"Well it's the same thing for truth, for what *is,* for what makes sense of life. That's what he's getting at, see? And sometimes you *get it,* the truth shines through, and your head lights up and you think, Wow!"

"Cool."

"And then the second part. When you hit that riff, you just want to stay in it, live it, right? For that moment, that's all you want."

"Yeah!"

"More than the ways of the flesh and the dross of the world."

"What is that, *dross?*"

"Garbage. Worthless stuff. See, what he's saying is that when you get that riff, or hit on that truth, even the very best weed in the world can't compare. You'd stop getting baked if you could keep on having that feeling."

C Dog went into a long silence. The thoughts seemed to be knocking around in his head.

"Tell you what," I said. "You keep this book. You have an assignment. To read the first two chapters. Think you can do that?"

"It's thick."

"That's not what I asked."

"I'll try," he said.

"Do or do not," I said. "There is no try."

In the morning I went to see Ira. He keeps office hours at Temple Beth Shalom two days a week, offering free legal advice to the poor. When there's no client, he talks to anyone who cares to stop by, especially if it's to debate some point of religion or philosophy.

Especially his friend, Saul Cohen. Saul was in his mid-seventies, slight of build, with a shock of Albert Einstein hair. I knew Saul. Once upon a time Ira bought Saul's 1980 Dodge Aspen so I'd have something to drive around L.A. That car, which Saul had lovingly cared for, ended up in flames courtesy of a couple of firebug thugs.

Saul did not know this.

And when I came through the door of the office the first thing Saul said was, "So how's the car running?"

From his wheelchair, Ira looked at me with an expression that said. *Tread carefully.*

"She's firing on all cylinders," I said.

Ira almost punched me.

"Ah, didn't I tell you?" Saul said. "So you like her?"

"She's one hot car," I said.

"Do you have a reason for being here, Michael?" Ira said.

"Were you able to find anything on Rory O'Connor?" I said.

"Who is this?" Saul said.

"This is business, Saul," Ira said.

"Ha. Business. Let me tell this Mr. Smarty Pants here, with the tattoo on his arm, there's more to life than business."

"Do tell," I said.

"Pretty girls," Saul said. "Eh? You got yourself a pretty girl?"

Ira said, "Saul—"

"What?" Saul said. "The man can't answer a simple question?"

"I'm kind of free at the moment," I said.

"You listen to me," Saul said. "Go out and find yourself a pretty girl. Get married. Before it's too late. Before you turn into an old no-goodnik."

"That's enough, Saul," Ira said. "I'll talk to your credit card company. Right now I need to talk to Michael."

"Fine!" Saul said. "I'll go out and take a look at my baby again."

"Um," I said, "I didn't drive it over here. I drove my Mustang."

"Mustang!" Saul said. "You some kind of fancy car collector or something? You don't like my Dodge?"

"Not so," I said. "Whenever I think about your Dodge it gives me a very warm feeling."

Saul smiled.

Ira frowned.

"Okay," Saul said, "you talk your fancy business. I'm going to go find me a pretty girl."

"Make sure she's over seventy," Ira said.

After Saul closed the door I said, "Am I an old no-goodnik?"

"You may be on your way," Ira said. "Which is why God has put me in your life."

"How do you know it isn't the other way around?"

"Because I've already paid for my sins," Ira said. "Any other questions?"

"You wanted to tell me something the other day," I said.

"I always want to tell you something, it seems."

"About me running away."

"Ah."

"Go ahead."

"You want?"

"No. But maybe ... go ahead."

"May I ask why the change?"

I shrugged. "Maybe it's the guy at the beach, C Dog."

"How so?"

"You want a laugh?" I said.

"I can always use one," Ira said.

"I'm trying to help him. Teach him. How to think, how to live. But who am I to do that?"

"I'm not laughing, Michael. I know you believe what's tattooed on your arm."

"That's an easy thing to do."

"Everyone needs a North Star. Keep following it."

"It's dark on the street right now," I said.

"Not completely," Ira said. "There are street lights. And by them you can read the signs, if you'll only bother to look. But you seem determined to keep your head down. Are you afraid of what you'll find?"

"Afraid?"

"The biggest fear a man has is finding out who he really is. You're not really Mike Romeo."

"I am now."

"But Michael Chamberlain is still inside you."

When he used my real name, my childhood name, it hit me like

a right cross. Because he was right. The me I once was and who
had killed a man in New Haven, and who had run away and
become quite another man, that me still had unresolved business.

"Michael," Ira said softly. "There is an old story about a village
glassblower. He has set up some of his work on a shelf outside his
shop. One day a poor villager walks by the shop, and is careless
with his walking stick. The stick knocks over many of the glass
figurines, and they shatter. The glassblower comes out and takes
hold of the man. 'I know you are poor,' he says, 'and there is no
hope of restitution. But now you must come inside and see what
you have destroyed.' He brings the man into the shop and shows
him all the beautiful figurines."

"I hope the guy left his walking stick outside," I said.

"Aha, there it is," Ira said. "That tongue of yours, always
seeking to deflect. That's your walking stick, Michael."

I pondered the thought. As is usual with Ira, even something
cryptic seems to make perfect sense. I wanted to walk out. Which
I knew was Ira's point.

Ira said, "You have shattered glass inside you. What you need
to see is the handiwork of the glassblower."

I said, "What I need is what you found on Rory O'Connor."

Ira wheeled over to the desk where his laptop was and punched
something up. "Rory O'Connor. Did two years on a four-year
felony pop. Possession for sale. Meth. He's on parole. About your
size. Six-four, two-thirty."

"That could be thirty pounds of fat," I said.

"Such things don't interest me," Ira said "So we have a name,
address, and record here. What we don't have is any connection to
Missy Nolan or Archie Jennison, other than the speculations of a
young lady you say can beat up men."

"Most men," I said. "Present company excluded."

"Regardless, unless we find such a connection, this seems like a
fool's errand."

"Then it's perfect for me," I said. "Better to be a fool than a no-
goodnik."

. . .

R ory O'Connor lived out in Canoga Park. The Walmart where Derinda Tyman worked was only a mile away. I decided to try her first.

It wasn't hard to spot her. Tall with pink hair. She was putting Pringles cans on a shelf.

"Hello, Derinda," I said.

She smiled, no doubt figuring I'd homed in on her giant name badge.

"May I help you?" she said.

"I think you can," I said, turning on the charm, which for me falls somewhere between Cary Grant and a brontosaurus.

"Great," she said.

"My name's Mike."

"Hi, Mike. What are you looking for?"

"The truth," I said.

She frowned.

I said, "I'm an investigator, and I don't want to upset you. But this is about the murder of Missy Nolan."

A dark cloud fell over her face. She looked around as if to see if anyone was listening.

"Why are you talking to me?" she said, lowering her voice.

"It has to do with Rory," I said.

She put her hand on her chest.

"Nothing to worry about," I said. "I'm trying to talk to as many people who knew Missy as I can."

"Why?"

"Trying to find out what happened. I understand Rory knew her, and maybe he could direct me to some people to talk to."

"But they have the guy," Derinda said. "Archie Jennison. You know that, don't you?"

"I sure do," I said.

"So why are you doing this?"

"I think there's some doubt that he did it is all," I said.

"Are you with the police?"

"No. I work for the lawyer representing Archie."

"Oh." She seemed a bit relieved. That lasted one second. "Who told you about Rory?"

"I don't want to cause him any trouble or concern," I lied. "I know he's out on parole, so I just want to keep things on the down low and ask him a couple of questions."

"He doesn't know anything," she said.

"I haven't asked yet," I said.

"Who gave you my name?" she said.

"I'm a careful guy," I said, basking in ambiguity.

"This is really creepy."

"Believe me, I know it is." I got one of Ira's cards and handed it to her. "Everything's so public these days. I don't like it one bit. But I have to do my job."

She looked around again. "I have to get back to work."

"Tell you what," I said. "You have a break coming up?"

"Maybe."

"Let me buy you a Coke. Or a snack. I'll wait for you at the Mickey D's."

She glanced at the card, back at me. "I don't know."

"Five minutes," I said. "You'll be doing me a favor."

She shook her head, hesitating.

"Did you know Missy?" I said.

"A little," she said.

"Five minutes. That's all I ask."

The McDonald's took up a corner of Walmart. It was open air, but still had that McDonald's smell—fries, coffee, cleaning solution. I was hungry and thought about ordering an Egg McMuffin. But because I thought about it, I didn't order it.

I got a medium coffee and sat in one of the half booths that gave me a view of a couple of yellow Caution *Cuidado* Wet Floor *Piso Mojado* towers and the display of Hickory Farms Meat &

Cheese platters in the aisle. I tried to imagine I was in an outdoor café in Paris. It didn't work.

A couple of well-seasoned gents were in the booth in front of me, conducting a spirited discussion.

"Never shoulda let 'em start voting," one said, in a volume that suggested the other was wearing a hearing aid.

"Ah, it's not so bad," the other said, in a volume that suggested he thought everyone in the place was wearing a hearing aid.

"So bad? We got no guts in this country anymore! Women want to be liked, that's all, that's how they vote! You gotta be nicey-nicey with terrorists. Look at Germany!"

"Who needs war?"

"War is all we get in this life. You want to survive? Don't let women vote!"

I wondered what she of the Queen Bodica tat would have to say to these gentlemen. And once I was on the subject of Malita Faust, I sat there with it for awhile.

My coffee was half finished when Derinda Tyman slid into the booth.

"Can I buy you something?" I said.

She shook her head. "You said five minutes."

"Did you call Rory?" I said.

Shook her head again. If she knew something, or suspected me for ulterior motives, I couldn't read it in her face.

"Okay, I thought maybe you could set up a meeting for me with him. Just to ask a few questions."

"I don't think he'd like that," she said.

"Why not?"

"He's very private."

"Most guys who do time are that way," I said.

"Did you?"

"Did I what?"

"Do time."

"Only a brief stint or two," I said.

"You look like somebody who might've."

"I try to be nice."

She said, "I'm sorry about what happened to Missy. That really bites."

I nodded.

"Why are they talking so loud?" She looked behind her at the codgers. I think they had moved on to discussing Lindberg.

"Why don't you give it a try?" I said. "I can't speak for my employer, but he could try to get through to Rory via his parole officer."

"Really?"

"It's not necessary. Can you give Rory a call and see if he'll talk to me?"

She sighed. Then told me to wait a moment. She took out her phone and stood over by the Hickory Farms display as she spoke.

The oldsters were on the subject of the breakdown of internal organs. I wanted to get out of there fast.

Derinda came back. "Okay," she said. "But he'll only talk in a public place."

"Fine with me."

"He's going to McGreevy's to watch the Lakers game. He said he'll talk to you there."

"That works for me. Thank you."

"Keep being nice," she said.

That left me about six hours to redeem. I don't kill time. Time is innocent. Relentless, sure. But it doesn't deserve to die. I wish it would slow down sometimes. Especially when you're not sure what's going on around you.

I drove over to a branch of the Los Angeles Public Library on Victory Boulevard. It was small and quiet and neat. Not too crowded. An old man sat in one of the soft wingback chairs by the magazine rack, reading an actual newspaper. I thought that was quaint.

I browsed the history section and selected a volume on

Churchill. I took it to a chair by the window facing the street. An Asian girl about sixteen sat at a table nearby, looking at an open book and writing notes with a pen on actual paper. I thought that was quaint, too.

Then I happened to glance over at the children's section, and saw a girl around ten reading a book to a boy who was maybe four. She was showing him the pictures, then turned the book around and read some of the words. She was in a small chair. The boy sat cross-legged on the floor in rapt attention.

And I thought, if there is any hope for this world, there it was. Passing on a love of reading and good books. I thought of C Dog then, hoping he'd get hooked on books. Yeah, I was starting him at a high level. But I was ten when I first read *The Story of Philosophy*. While most of my contemporaries were playing Super Mario Brothers, I was in my room reading Will Durant. I didn't go to many parties. In fact, I didn't go to any parties. I was not invited to other kids' homes. If you looked up the word *dweeb* in a dictionary in those days, my picture would have been there.

It was books that saved me. My mom took me to the public library in New Haven when I was seven and I got a library card. It felt like I was being ushered into the kingdom of all knowledge. I would go there sometimes and just walk among the stacks looking at the books and thinking, how can I ever know what is in all these books? I would like to know. I would like to dive into these books and stay there forever.

So big sister and little brother, read on. May you someday find Dickens and Melville and Jane Austen and Chandler and Plato and *To Kill a Mockingbird* and *The Brothers Karamazov* and *Fahrenheit 451*. Maybe you'll write your own books someday, if writing is not outlawed by the AI running the planet.

For the next couple of hours I followed Churchill from the disaster of the Dardanelles to the miracle of Dunkirk. He traded barbs with Clement Attlee ("A modest man with much to be modest about") and the formidable Lady Nancy Astor, Britain's first female Member of Parliament. At a dinner party she leaned over and said, "Winston, if I were your wife I would poison your coffee." Churchill replied, "Nancy, if I were your husband, I'd drink it."

As the world of social media drowns in its own bile, wit abides.

McGreevy's was a sports bar in Van Nuys. Wood and brass inside, high tables and chairs, and a long bar. Big screen TVs throughout and a pool table in the corner. The bartenders wore long black vests and the waitresses wore short black skirts. The place was about half full and everybody seemed engaged in some kind of conversation or good-natured argument. The Lakers game was on three of the TVs.

Rory O'Connor was sitting at a high table, alone, watching the Lakers on the TV above the bar. He had a glass of beer and a basket of tortilla chips in front of him. He didn't notice my approach.

"Rory?"

He turned his head and looked at me with heavy-lidded eyes like Robert Mitchum in *Cape Fear*.

I parked myself on the other stool at the table.

"Nobody asked you to sit," Rory O'Connor said. His voice was a little high for his brooding look. I could imagine that getting him into a lot of fights in prison.

"Excuse my impertinence," I said.

"Your what?"

"My insolence."

He said that if I was effing with him he was going to shove the pepper shaker into a place on my body that was not designed to house pepper shakers.

"No need for that," I said. "I sometimes fall into my college vocabulary."

"Ask me if I care."

"I'll save us time and assume you don't," I said. "I'm just here for a few questions, and then I'll be on my way."

"Derinda said it has something to do with that killing."

"You know Archie Jennison?" I asked.

"No."

"Missy Nolan?"

"No."

"Not even a little?"

"No. We done?"

"Why? I'm enjoying this conversation. A lot of depth."

"All right," he said. "I'm done. See ya."

He waited for me to get up. I didn't.

"Go," he said.

"I think I'll stay," I said.

He paused. Half smiled. "You don't want to go there with me."

"But I like there. It's very nice this this time of year. The leaves are turning. Let's go there together."

"You want to go outside?" Rory said.

"If you come with me," I said. "But I do want to let you know something."

He waited.

I said, "If we do go outside, I will make you cry. And then I'll break your fingers. Which I don't want to do, because you'll need them to dry your tears."

He kept looking at me.

"Or you can sit and listen to my theory," I said. "And then make an informed decision about what to do about it."

He picked up the pepper shaker and held it like a joystick.

"So?" he said.

"So I think you did know Missy Nolan. I think you sold her methamphetamine before you got sent up. And it would be very easy to check court records and the DA's office to see if Missy's name shows up in proximity to yours. How'm I doing?"

He didn't move for a moment. Gears clicked in his head. I could hear them. I knew what he was going to do before he did.

He slid off his chair, slowly, trying to lull me into a false sense of security. I was reading him like a large-print book.

So when he shot his right fist out, still holding the pepper shaker—which would make his fist feel like a sledge—my left hand intercepted the blow. Then I slammed his wrist on the edge of the table. The pepper shaker came loose and I grabbed it with my right hand.

As Rory O'Connor grunted and took hold of his wrist with his free hand, I replaced the pepper next to the salt and said, "Somebody may want that."

He held his wrist and swore at me.

Which is when Derinda Tyman swooped over. I hadn't seen her come in.

"Rory!" she said. "You said you wouldn't."

"Get outta here!" he said.

"Stay," I said. Because I noticed something very interesting about Derinda. Very interesting indeed.

She was wearing a turquoise necklace, one that clacked when she moved.

A large bartender, which was apparently the only kind they had in this place, came over and said, "We don't want any trouble here. You guys cool?"

"We had a slight disagreement about seasonings," I said. "That's over now."

Rory just stared.

"It's okay," Derinda said.

"Make sure it is," the bartender said and returned to his duties behind the bar.

I said, "Can I buy you a beer?"

Rory looked like he wanted to jump out of his skin and whack me with his arm bones. Derinda put her arm around his shoulder and said to me, "Can't you just go now?"

"It's up to him," I said.

Rory said something unkind.

"I hope you two will be very happy together," I said.

· · ·

Outside in the parking lot I called Kathy Nolan.

"I realize this is late," I said, "but do you think you can drive over to the Valley? I'm at a place called McGreevy's, it's a sports bar at Van Nuys and Roscoe. I may have something here that will help us both get closure on Missy."

"What do you mean by that?" Her voice was thick.

"Are you able to drive?" I said.

"What, you think I'm drunk or something?"

"I don't want you driving if you are."

"I am perfectly capable of driving."

I hoped she was.

I called Ira. "Can you get ahold of the lead detective handling the murder? Whatsisname?"

"Waring." Ira said, "I'm sure I can."

"Then do it, please."

"Now?"

"Now. I'm at a sports bar in the Valley, McGreevy's. On Van Nuys. I've got the deliverance for our client. The Red Sea is parting."

"What is it, Michael?"

"Tell him I've got relevant evidence and a witness he needs to talk to."

"Who?"

"Time is of the essence," I said.

"Are you going to explain this to me?" Ira said.

"Not now."

"Michael, if I get this detective to move, for which there is no guarantee, he is going to want to know why."

"Tell him to trust me," I said.

"That will be a hard sell," Ira said.

"Which is what you're good at," I said, and hung up.

· · ·

Now it was a matter of waiting. I slipped back into McGreevy's and took a table where I could watch Rory and Delinda. She looked like she was trying to comfort him. He looked like he didn't want to be comforted. He kept shaking her hand off him. At least they ordered another round of beer.

I nursed a Corona and watched some of the Lakers game. The Lakers were in a rebuilding program after the retirement of Kobe Bryant. They were young and looked like they had some swagger. It would take some time to overtake the Warriors, who looked to be dominant for several more years.

The sports bar is the new Church of the Hot-Blooded Male. Communion is not by wine and wafer, but by beer and buffalo wing. The priests are the bartenders. They will hear your confession and offer you absolution by way of Absolut. You perform an act of penance by buying a round of drinks. In place of a crucifix is a big-screen TV. You don't pray, you cheer. Your comfort does not come from knowing the will of God. It comes from knowing the stats of your favorite team.

My waitress came by and asked me if I'd like another beer. Mine was only half gone, but at the Church of the HBM it is sacrilegious to allow the communion cups—bottles—to reach empty without the offer of another. I told her thanks, but I was okay for now.

Ira texted me. He said the detective, Alderson, was coming to the bar, and that *He is not happy*.

Apparently, it was not my lot in life to make others happy.

Twenty minutes went by. Then Rory and Derinda got up and started for the front door.

I caught up with them as they headed across the dimly lit parking lot. There were cars in just about every space.

"I can't let you go just yet," I said.

"Get outta my way!" Rory said.

"Can't," I said.

"Don't fight!" Derinda said.

"Listen to her," I said. "You don't want to do this."

"Derinda, call the cops," he said.

"They're already on their way," I said.

Rory said, "What is this?"

"I'm detaining you," I said. "This is sort of a citizen's arrest."

He put his forearm in my chest and pushed. I took his forearm and twisted it behind his body.

"Let him go!" Derinda said.

"You have the right to remain silent," I said. "Anything you say might make me mad."

He tried to move but I had him in complete control.

"You can't do this!" Derinda said.

"You mean physically or legally?" I said, just to keep the conversation flowing.

"Let him go!"

"You can sue me later," I said.

Rory tried to kick me, so I folded him over the trunk of a car. I think it was a Buick.

"Stop!" Derinda said.

With impeccable timing, a black-and-white cop cruiser pulled into the parking lot and blurted its siren.

Two patrol officers, a man and a woman, got out. The man came toward us while the woman took a position off to the side. The woman wore a body cam.

"What goes on here?" the male officer said.

"He's threatening us!" Derinda said, pointing at me.

"This is a detention, officer," I said. "A homicide detective from the west side is on his way."

"Homicide? Why?"

"To question these two," I said.

"What!" Rory said.

"All right," the officer said. "Calm down. First off, I want to see IDs from each of you."

"We didn't do anything!" Derinda said.

"Ma'am, please step over to Officer Espejo. You two stay right here."

"You can't do this!" Derinda said.

"Please, ma'am."

Derinda reached into her purse, pulled out her phone. "I'm recording this!"

"Put the phone away, ma'am."

"I have a right!"

"You're being detained, ma'am. You don't have a right."

Rory said, "We're gonna sue everybody here."

The officer said, "Put the phone back in your purse or I will confiscate it."

"No way!" Derinda said.

"I'll have to put you in handcuffs if you don't comply," he said.

"You can't do that either!" she said.

I said, "Actually, he can. Officer safety."

"Thank you," the officer said. I caught his name badge in the sparse light. *Shields.*

Derinda took a step back and activated her phone camera, held it up. The officer said, "Put your hands down, ma'am."

"I am being harassed!" Derinda said. "Police harassment!"

Her outrage overpowered her sense of observation. Officer Espejo came at her from behind, reached around, and snatched the phone out of Derinda's hand. With one smooth move the officer twisted Derinda's arm behind her and slapped a silver cuff on her wrist.

Rory took a step toward her. Officer Shields put his hand on Rory's chest.

"Stay right there," Officer Shields said.

Officer Espejo got Derinda's other arm behind her and attached the other cuff.

"Everybody chill," said Shields. "We're going to clear this up."

"Nothin' to clear up!" Rory said. "This psycho attacked me inside and now he's doing this!"

"What's this about an attack?" Officer Shields said.

"I felt I was being threatened by a pepper shaker," I said.

"A what?"

"A glass receptacle as weapon," I said. "I'm sure if we go inside we can find a witness or two."

"Hold on," Shields said. "Is that what this is about?"

"No, officer," I said. "It's about much more. Do you know a homicide detective on the west side, name of Waring?"

"No," said Officer Shields.

"He's coming here to talk to these two," I said.

"What is this?" Rory said.

Derinda shouted something that was not nice.

Shields said, "You are all being detained. You two turn around and place your hands on the trunk of the car."

Rory said something that sounded like his own trucking company couldn't believe this was happening.

We put our hands on the trunk and got patted down. Then Officer Shields told all of us to sit on the pavement. Officer Espejo brought the shackled Derinda over to where we were and we all sat down like little campers.

"What shall we talk about?" I said.

Rory and Derinda shared their opinions simultaneously, disavowing any interest in further conversation.

We stayed like that for another couple of minutes. Finally, Officer Shields came to us and said, "Detective Waring is en route. So we're all going to wait for him."

"I'm expecting one other person," I said.

"What?"

"Her name is Kathy Nolan," I said. "She's part of this gathering. An important part."

"This better be good," Shields said.

"I've heard that before," I said.

"While we wait," said Shields, "let's check IDs."

. . .

W aring arrived fifteen minutes later. The detective was sharply dressed, as neat as a new shaving kit. Khaki trousers, blue blazer, light blue shirt. He wore his detective shield on his chest. He had a partner with him, a younger guy, not so neatly dressed. He was introduced as Detective Goodridge.

By this time Derinda Tyman was seated in the back of the black-and-white. A small crowd had started to gather. Officer Shields shooed them away. Rory and I were still seated on the asphalt.

With his finger, Waring motioned me over to him. When I got there he said, "This is your call, so make it. And make it good or I'm going to run you in just to relieve my headache."

"Still waiting on one more arrival," I said.

"Tell me exactly why I am here."

"I don't want to ruin the dramatic effect," I said.

"You better tell me right now," Waring said.

"I'll give you the set up," I said. "You have a circumstantial case against Archie Jennison for the Nolan killing. I am going to hand you evidence that points in another direction. But I don't want to say anything yet because that could mess up what the witnesses say."

"I heard about you," Waring said.

"I hope it was about how honest I am."

"You're a nutcase," Waring said. "You talk like you're some college professor and nobody knows that much about you. You've got some kills, too."

"Since you're a detective," I said, "you probably also know those were justifiable homicides, no charges filed."

"Yeah," he said, "but it doesn't make you exactly the best guy to be around."

"I'm trying to help you out," I said.

"We'll see," he said. "Right now I got a woman in custody for resisting, and a parolee who hasn't done anything I know of, and your word. If this doesn't work out to something, I'm going to be hearing about it."

"On the other hand," I said, "you might turn out to be a hero."

K athy Nolan finally made it. She lit a cigarette the moment she got out of her car.

I introduced her to Waring.

Waring looked at me, waiting.

I said, "I met Kathy at Missy's apartment."

"Jennison's apartment?" Waring said.

"Yes. She wanted to gather up some of Missy's things. One thing she wanted wasn't there. It was a necklace, a turquoise necklace."

"Did you find it?" Kathy said.

"Let's find out," I said. I walked toward the patrol car, motioning for Waring and Kathy to follow.

"What is this?" Rory shouted.

Officer Espejo opened the rear door and motioned for Derinda to slide out. She was still cuffed behind the back.

Kathy gasped the moment Derinda's feet hit pavement.

"Is that it?" I said.

"Yes!" Kathy said, grabbing the necklace. "Take it off!"

Officer Espejo moved fast, jumped in, took Kathy by the wrist. "Let go, ma'am."

"It's Missy's!"

"Now!"

Kathy dropped her hand, burst into tears.

"All right," Waring said. "Explain this."

I said, "That necklace belonged to Missy Nolan. Her mother bought it for her. So you need to ask, detective, how it ended up on the chest of Rory O'Connor's girlfriend."

"This is bogus!" Rory shouted.

"Quiet!" Waring said. "Now, Mrs. Nolan, can you talk?"

Kathy wiped the tears from her eyes with the back of her right hand. She still held the lighted cigarette in her left.

"Yes," she said.

Waring said, "You've identified this necklace as your daughter's. Is there any way you can verify that?"

"There's an inscription on the back. It's in Navajo. I could never pronounce it. The first word is Ayoo, or something like that. The other word is something ishi. Please look!"

"Officer," Waring said, "will you please remove the necklace?"

Officer Espejo complied, handed the necklace to Waring.

Kathy was on one side of the detective, I was on the other.

"Behind that one," Kathy said, pointing to the large piece of turquoise in the middle.

Waring said, "Officer, shine your flashlight, please."

Flashlight came out, and the beam hit the necklace.

I saw the engraved script.

Ayóó Áníínishní.

T hey arrested Rory O'Connor and put a screaming Derinda Tyman in the back of another black and white to cool off. They told Kathy they needed to keep the necklace as evidence, but that she would certainly get it back when the case was concluded.

Waring told me I'd be getting a call from him soon, and then probably from a prosecutor. He said the same to Kathy Nolan. She looked completely spent.

Then we were alone in the parking lot.

"You okay to drive?" I said.

"I told you, I didn't have anything to drink," she said.

"I just meant by being tired. I could drive you home and pick you up tomorrow to come get your car."

"Why would you do that?" she said.

"Just to help out."

"What will happen to Archie?"

"He'll get out," I said. "Probably tomorrow."

"I still wish Missy never went with him."

She got a cigarette and lit it. "I can drive. Thank you for looking out for me."

"Take care," I said.

O n Monday night Zane Donahue threw a party for the newly sprung Archie Jennison.

Featured guest was the intrepid investigator Mike Romeo, hero of the hour. Ira was invited but preferred to spend the evening with a volume of Kipling's verse. I would have joined him, except there was something stuck in my craw. It's good to check your craw every once in awhile.

Besides, I knew someone was going to be here that I wanted to see again.

Malita Faust was on the other side of Zane Donahue's cavernous living room. She was wearing an off-the-shoulder red dress that would have stopped a Roman chariot race.

A couple dozen people milled around, holding drinks. I recognized several from the pool party. Only now they dressed like beautiful people trying to impress all the other beautiful people.

When Malita saw me she cut a swath through the crowd. Smiling, she grabbed my arm, pulled me to her and kissed my cheek.

"Baby," she said.

I caught the barest whiff of perfume, but it created pictures in my mind of Scheherazade and the Arabian Nights. I, on the other hand, wore my only sport coat, a herringbone job, over my cleanest polo shirt. I was not exactly a dazzling prince.

"Looks like quite a soiree," I said.

"For you and Archie," Malita said. "We're all so happy. We knew you could do it."

"Uh-huh."

She took a step back. "What's that mean?"

"It means, *Uh-huh*."

Frowning, she said, "I think we need to talk about this."

"Sure."

"But not here. I'm taking you to dinner. You took me to the burger place, I have another place in mind for us. You in?"

"If I say no, will you kick my ribs?"

"Yes."

"Then, sure," I said. "Let's do dinner."

"I'll set it up. Meantime—"

"Mike!" Archie Jennison flew across the room to me. His voice had stopped all conversation.

A few of the people started to applaud.

For me.

Archie pumped my hand. "How you doin', boy? You are the man."

"I'm one of them," I said.

"All man," Malita said.

"You never lost faith in me," Archie said. "Even though I treated you like ... well, you know."

"I know," I said.

He had a big smile on his face. "Hey, what are you drinking?"

"A beer is fine," I said.

"You stay right here."

"I'll watch him," Malita said.

"You'll have to share!" Behind us, Princess Moira had suddenly appeared. She was dressed in something black and billowing, with a string of pearls around her neck. Heavy on the makeup.

"Hands off," Malita said. "He's mine."

"We'll just see about that," the princess said.

"Please, ladies," I said. "I'm not just some choice piece of beef. I have a mind, too."

"Do we care?" Malita asked Princess Moira.

"Not a bit," the princess said.

We went around and around like that until Archie came back with a bottle of Guinness. And a welcome message.

"Mr. Donahue would like to see you in his office," Archie said.

. . .

Z ane Donahue was dressed in a black shirt open at the collar, black slacks and a white sport coat. He looked like Bogie on casual night in Casablanca. He greeted me by offering a cigar from his humidor. This time I took one and stuck it in the pocket of my sport coat.

"Don't want to join me?" he said, taking one of the stogies and preparing to cut it.

"Not sure how long I'll be staying," I said.

"Oh? Why is that?"

"I don't really go in for celebrity status stuff."

Donahue finished his surgery and lit his cigar with a butane flame. Through a puff of smoke he said, "But you are the man."

"Everybody keeps reminding me," I said. "I'm starting to have a self-image crisis."

"I doubt that," Donahue said.

"So what did you want to see me about?"

"You know. Change your mind about coming to work for me, fight for me."

"I thought I made it clear."

"Nothing is ever clear," Donahue said. "You're a smart guy, you know that. After all that philosophy, is anything really clear?"

He had a point. But I was not about to concede it.

"Here," he said, and pulled out some folded bills from his pants pocket. He tucked them in my coat pocket, next to the premium cigar. "A little token of my thanks, for getting Archie out of the can. Take your girl out to dinner with it."

"My girl?"

He smiled. "She's quite a firecracker, isn't she?"

"I think you may be jumping the gun," I said.

"I know what I see, and there's electricity in the air," he said.

I fished out the bills. There were five of them. All with Ben Franklin on the front. I tossed the bills on his desk.

"I'll pay my own way," I said.

"You against success or something?" Donahue said.

"Against obligations," I said. "And by the way, if I walk out of here, is that pug of yours going to get in my face again?"

With a laugh Donahue said, "Casey wasn't invited tonight. Only people of fine breeding."

"Thanks for the cigar," I said.

"There's plenty more," Donahue said, "if you ever get a hankering."

Back in the party room I was happy to see Malita and the princess occupied with others. Archie was at the bar. He was talking to that gray-haired man, with the patch. The one I'd seen in court at his arraignment. He saw me looking at him. His eye did not look friendly.

Then Archie followed his gaze and saw me and practically knocked people over to get to where I was.

"Let me get you another brewski," Archie said. His face was flushed.

"Still nursing," I said.

"Then how about something else? How'd you like a little female companionship tonight?"

"Come on, Arch."

"What?"

"Pimping?"

"Aw Mike, just trying to get you what you deserve."

"When is Missy's funeral?" I said.

"Huh?"

"You don't seem all that broken up about her death."

He snorted a laugh, a singularly inappropriate noise. "Sure I am," he said. "She was a good kid."

"That it?" I said. "All you can say?"

"What do you want me to say, Mike?" He straightened himself up. "Of course I'm sorry! But life goes on, you know?"

I took a sip of my Guinness and then said, "Why would Rory O'Connor want to kill her?"

The plastic smile on Archie's face faded. He shrugged. "He's a scumbag. What else do you have to know?"

"Even a scumbag has to have a motive."

"What do you even care?" Some red lightning flashed in Archie's eyes. I tensed because I've seen that look in many eyes before. It usually means a fist is coming my way. The change in Archie was as quick as it was irrational.

And then there was Malita, jumping into the middle of the two of us, saying, "Boys, what's the beef here?"

"Nothin'!" Archie said. He went back across the room. This time he bumped two people.

"What's up with him?" Malita said.

"Too much to drink," I said.

"Oh?" She put a hand on my chest. "You didn't bait him or anything?"

"He didn't need baiting," I said.

"He's on the edge enough as it is."

"What are you, his sister?"

"Mike ..."

"I'm taking off." I put my half-full beer bottle—or half-empty, if you're an existentialist—on a table.

"But we haven't made our date yet," Malita said.

"Have your people call my people," I said, and walked out.

Honor, wrote Montaigne, is not a matter of praise from without, but from the ability to look within, "where no eyes can pierce but our own." It's why a true champion will not accept a victory based on cheating. Or being duped.

As I got in Spinoza I tipped the rearview mirror down so I could look in my own eyes. The moment I made contact I knew something was off. I just didn't know what. Which is not a good feeling. It's like the howl of a wolf in a classic horror movie. It makes your skin crawl over your bones and you freeze, not knowing which way to turn, which way to run.

I told myself that my duty was done. Ira and I had defended

Archie Jennison on a murder charge. That charge was now dropped. Job over.

Except I couldn't get that wolf howl out of my mind. And I knew that sooner or later I'd have to track it down, or it would keep on howling, keep on haunting me through the night.

The next morning, as I was doing pushups on the beach, C Dog walked up to me holding *The Story of Philosophy*. He threw it on the sand in front of me.

"What's up?" I said.

"Take it back. I can't do it."

"Can't do what?"

"I tried, man! I don't care, I'm calling you *man*."

I got into a sitting position. "What's wrong?"

"I can't understand it! It's too ... I just don't get it!"

He sounded really sad about it, not angry.

"Sit down," I said.

C Dog dropped to the sand, shaking his head.

"I know this is all new to you," I said.

"I don't read good!"

"It's a matter of practice, C. You get better at it. But only if you don't give up."

"Too many big words."

"So what?" I said. "Life has too many big problems. You going to fold up?"

C Dog poked his finger in the sand.

"Have you ever heard of a dictionary?" I said.

"Of course."

"Do you have one?"

"No."

"Did you know they have them online? For free."

"Yeah, yeah."

"Then use it. Plow through. Look up the words you don't know, then read the paragraph again. And then after you read the paragraph, think about it. Think about what it might mean to you."

"Why can't you just tell me what to do?"

"Because then you'll be a puppet on a string," I said. I picked up the book and tossed it on his lap. "You were not made to be a puppet."

I was getting dressed after my shower when my phone buzzed. My whitelist showed the name. Lauren.

"Mike Romeo," I said.

"Um ..."

"How can I help you, Lauren?"

"I'm scared."

"What's wrong?"

"Can you meet me?"

"Where are you?"

"I'm going to take the bus to Hollywood. Can you meet me there?"

"I can come to you."

"No. Please."

"Where in Hollywood?"

"There's a souvenir shop on the corner of Hollywood and Cherokee. I'll be there. It'll probably take me an hour and a half."

"I'll be there," I said.

She was in the T-shirt section of the store, next to some glittery, hot-pink shirts emblazoned with the sentiment *I May Live in the Midwest, But This Girl is Hollywood.*

"Thank you," she said. "I didn't want anybody to see me with you."

"Why this place?" I said.

"I used to come here a lot when I was in high school," she said. "I guess you can tell I don't get out much."

"What did you want to see me about?"

"I need to tell you something but I don't want to be involved. Can you promise me I won't be?"

"I should tell you something first," I said. "The client I was working for, Archie Jennison, he's been released. There's nothing left to get involved in."

"There might be. I don't want to get dragged in. I'm afraid of these people."

"What people?"

"Who kill people," she said.

"Does this have anything to do with Archie?"

"I'm afraid of him, too. I don't know. I just feel like I have to tell you something. I don't want to go to the police. If I have to go to the police I won't tell you."

"Lauren, unless this affects my client, which you say it does not, then I can't make you go to the cops. I can advise you. I can encourage you. But if you don't want to go you don't have to. Only . . ."

"What?"

"If you have information that can help in the administration of justice, and don't let the authorities know, it might haunt you."

She closed her eyes then, took a deep breath.

"Maybe you could do something," she said.

"Like what?"

"Like go to the police for me."

"Why don't you tell me what it is you have, and I'll advise you. How does that sound?"

She paused and picked up a snow globe with a little Hollywood sign in it.

She said, "They arrested a guy for the killing. O'Connor?"

"Right," I said. "Rory O'Connor."

"I saw his picture on the internet. He isn't the one who did it."

A group of Asian tourists came into the shop, laughing and pointing. One of the men took pictures with a nice-sized camera, to make sure the folks back home got a good look at the real

Hollywood. Like the man said, if you look under the phony tinsel of Hollywood you find the real tinsel underneath.

Only I was dealing with a real bombshell.

"How do you know this?" I asked.

"Because I saw who did it," she said. "I was in the laundry room. It was late, I turned off the light. I was sitting there in the dark. I do that sometimes. Just to rest. After about ten minutes or so, I saw something move. You can see the stairwell door from the laundry room. It was the door opening. Slowly. Then a man stuck his head out. I only saw the back of him. He walked out through the back exit."

"Walked?"

"Like everything was fine."

"You didn't see his face?"

She shook her head. "But it wasn't the man they arrested. The build and hair were totally different."

"Tell me about that."

"He had curly hair and was big, like a weight lifter."

"Curly hair?"

"Kind of frizzy and curly."

"What color?"

She thought about it. "It was hard to tell in the light."

"Best guess."

"I thought maybe a little reddish."

"You didn't see his face?"

"Uh-uh. There's supposed to be a security camera out there, but it's not working."

"Terrific."

"I know, right?" She looked at the floor. "I should have told the police."

"I'll tell them," I said.

"But then they'll know!"

I couldn't blame her for her fear. Thugs threatening or even killing witnesses is a reality in any big city.

"How about I don't tell the police anything. Yet. Until I try a couple of things myself."

"Things?"

I nodded.

"Legal things?" she said.

I shrugged.

I offered to drive her home but she said she liked taking the bus. So I waited with her at the bus stop and saw her off. Then I walked up Hollywood Boulevard toward the Chinese Theater. At Highland I crossed over to the other side of the boulevard and walked back toward the Egyptian. I was thinking about a guy I knew with curly, reddish hair. A fellow I affectionately called Die Scum. I thought about how I could prove he was the killer of Missy Nolan. I thought about how much I would enjoy doing that.

I kept walking. Now I was working up an appetite. Which was intentional. Because in a few hours I was going to be taken out to dinner.

"I'm going to seduce you tonight," Malita Faust said.

I'd just taken a sip of water and had to tamp down a spit take.

Malita smiled. She was sitting across from me at a window table in one of those high-end Santa Monica restaurants, you know, where the beef carpaccio starter is twice as much as a dinner for two at the Sizzler —and I'm including a fully stuffed baked potato in that calculation.

"Is that called the direct approach?" I said.

"Like it?"

"I feel ... tawdry," I said.

"What?"

"I have a mind, too!"

"Shut up," she said.

Malita's black, thin-strapped evening dress revealed smooth but substantial shoulders, with a dive down to just the right touch of alluring curvature. If she was serious about seduction, she was off to a great start.

"We both know how this is going to end," she said.

"Don't I get a say in this?"

"You don't want a say. You want *me*."

"What if I told you I want marriage and children and a little house with a picket fence?"

"Marriage is overrated," she said. "I was married once."

"Oh?"

"He left me."

"Sorry."

"Said he wanted someone more feminine." She sighed. "And he found him."

"Ah."

"Kind of messes with a woman's self-esteem, you know? So I don't need more rejection."

With timing out of an Oscar Wilde play, a waiter approached our table and asked if we would like to hear about the specials.

"I like anything hot," Malita said.

The waiter, who was probably twenty-five or so, did not pick up the amorous undertone. He did extol the pleasures of tonight's specials. "Roasted heirloom beet salad, herb-crusted Atlantic Cod, and for dessert the Crostata Di Fichi, a delicate polenta cake topped with caramelized figs, honey cream, and mascarpone gelato."

Then he asked if we wanted anything to drink.

Malita gave me the eye of the tigress.

"Double bourbon," I said. "And make it fast."

Malita ordered a glass of chardonnay.

"Now where were we?" she said.

"I think we were discussing the Smoot-Hawley Tariff Act," I said.

"Do you like me, Mike?"

"Sure."

"I mean, really?"

"Really liking requires more knowing," I said.

"Then let's get to know each other," she said. "And later we'll go to my place."

"I'm not that kind of a boy."

"You have something against sex?"

I cleared my throat.

"Don't you like sex?" she said.

"How 'bout those Lakers?" I said.

"You're not gay, are you? Please don't be gay."

"How about philosophy?"

"Huh?"

"Let's talk some philosophy."

She leaned back in her chair. "You are a buzz kill," she said.

"Don't knock philosophy," I said. "It will tell you that where a body—and let me tell you, you have a body—is made the object of sensual pleasure only, without regard to the communion of a soul and mind, true love cannot exist."

She looked at me for a long moment. "Where do you come up with this stuff?"

"I make it up and write it on walls," I said.

"If I didn't think you were so hot I might think you're weird."

"I am weird. And I'm not that hot."

"Oh yes you are. You're habanero sauce hot."

"I think of myself more as a mild cheddar."

"Look at me, Mike."

I looked.

She said, "I'm talking about having a good time, no questions asked."

"I always ask," I said.

The waiter came back with our drinks. Malita told him we needed more time to look at the menu.

Malita lifted her wine glass and said, "To good times."

I lifted my glass and said, *"Aequam servare mentem."*

"What the h—"

"It's Latin. It means keep an unruffled mind."

She shook her head. "Why do you talk like a college professor? Did you go to college?"

"I didn't finish."

"Why not?"

"Personal matters."

"Ooh, let's talk about those!" she said.

"Let's look at the menu," I said.

We got around to ordering and I cleverly managed to move the conversation in her direction. She was twenty-eight, went to high school in Orange County, had a doctor father and a massage thera-pist mother. She went to San Diego State for a year, got bored with school, dropped out, worked at Starbucks and Old Navy. She got into kickboxing to get herself in shape. Her trainer, a guy named Jack Faust, thought she had potential to be competitive and started to train her. Later on she married him. The marriage lasted a little over a year.

But her fighting took off. Which is when she caught the eye of Zane Donahue. He was going to take her to the "next level."

Our food arrived. Paella for Malita, sea bass for me. As Malita took her first bite, I said, "What exactly is your relationship with Zane Donahue?"

She chewed that one over. "Professional," she said. "Nothing else."

"Any reason Archie Jennison should be afraid of him?"

"Zane is a fair man. He's ruthless in business, that's all."

"How ruthless?"

"If Zane likes you, you've got nothing to worry about. And Zane likes you."

"Does he like Archie?"

"Are you ... you're not thinking Zane would have anything to do with ..."

"Just asking," I said. "Remember? That's what I do."

"Well don't ask," she said. "You've got a good thing going, don't spoil it."

"What good thing?"

"Zane," she said. "And me."

That was my cue to fork some of my sea bass.

Like my throat, it was a little dry.

A fter dinner we took a walk down to the beach. The pier was alive with music and lights. The air was crisp. Malita held my arm and kept her body close to mine.

We stopped near the water's edge and listened to the whisper of waves. The moon was an illuminated thumbnail over sea.

"Mike?"

"Hm?"

"This is your cue."

She released my arm and turned me to face her.

"You'll see," she said.

Malita Faust could not have set this up any better had she been a screenwriter.

Mike leans over and kisses Malita.

Fade Out.

F *ade in.*
    Malita's apartment. Night. Soft lights. Malita writhes in Mike's arms, plastering kisses on his neck and mouth. She pushes him and Mike falls back on her bed. Malita jumps on top of him and kisses him again. Then Malita speaks.

"Don't fight me."

Mike doesn't want to fight. He wants to jump off the cliff with her and plunge into the ocean below, no matter what's under the surface, no matter if he'll have to fight to keep breathing.

But just before he gives up and falls, he hears something in the distance. Way back in his brain, the part that is not now raging with fire.

What he hears is the howl of a wolf.

Mike speaks.

"Hold on."

Malita answers.

"Don't talk."

Malita attacks his mouth with hers, and the edge of the cliff gets closer. Mike realizes he better put the brakes on now or it's over and down, down, down.

Mike gives Malita a perfectly executed submission reversal move, as if they were in a cage. Malita ends up on her back, Mike on top holding her down.

Malita says, "Ooh, I like that."

Mike responds, "Stop trying so hard."

"What do you mean?"

"You want me to submit. And you're using every ancient weapon of your sex."

"Stop talking, Mike."

"You've been manipulating me all along. Ever since I bought you chili-cheese fries."

Malita's expression changes. Not in a good way.

"Get off me," Malita says.

"Not till you tell me who put you up to this."

Malita lets loose with a primal scream, and makes her own escape move. It's a good one. Mike ends up face down. Malita has a choke hold on him.

I didn't see this coming in the script.

Malita Faust was a champion, and she was inflicting damage. My windpipe was kinked. I'd be out in seconds.

Never hit a girl, my father taught me.

It's a rule I try to follow.

Unless I think I'm going to die.

That's when my elbows take on a life of their own.

I rammed a back shot to her ribs that would have dented a truck.

She *oomphed* and her hold loosened.

I flipped her on her back and held her down. She kept fighting to get up. She'd have made a good rodeo bull. But she wasn't going anywhere.

She did curse, though. She was very good at it. Finally, she paused for a breath.

"You finished?" I said.

She cursed and squirmed.

I put my forearm under her chin and pushed her mouth closed and her head back.

"You're finished now," I said. "You almost had me. All that beautiful music we could have made, as the poet says."

She stopped squirming. Her eyes submitted.

"You have something to say?" I released her chin.

"Will you get off me?" she said.

"Talk to me," I said.

"I can't," she said.

"Donahue put you up to all this, didn't he?"

"Please, Mike."

"Too easy," I said. "Derinda Tyman is in on this, too. Shows up with the evidence around her neck. You're both setting up Rory O'Connor."

She didn't answer. Her face did, though. It looked defeated.

I got off her and sat facing her. "You almost had me," I said.

Stroking her neck, Malita sat up with her back against the sofa.

We didn't say anything for a minute.

I said, "Tell me why Rory O'Connor's on the hook for this."

"I don't know," she said. Then, with more force, and looking me in the eye, she said, "You've got to believe me."

"Why?" I said. I got to my feet. She stayed on the floor, looking at her hands.

"I didn't want it to be this way," she said. "If that means anything."

"It doesn't," I said, and walked out.

Love builds a Heaven in Hell's despair, wrote Blake. I never did understand Blake, but he could turn a phrase. And that one seemed right as I drove up the coast in the night, top down, wind biting. L.A. was having a frosty snap, doing a bad imitation of Bangor, Maine. Perfect weather for Hell's despair.

Yes, she almost had me. Then came the oldest move in the book, Delilah's scissors, the betrayal. I should have seen it coming. But I hadn't wanted to. I liked Malita Faust. She had an elemental quality, an animal attractiveness, and could really scrap.

But she could also lie like a politician behind in the polls.

The Roman poet Catullus wrote, "I hate and love. You may ask why I do so. I do not know. But I feel it and am in torment."

Not much has changed, has it, Cat?

The next morning I went downtown to the jail for a walk-in visit with Rory O'Connor. I got the go-ahead from the desk and was led to the visiting room once more. O'Connor came in a minute later, sat opposite me and picked up the handset. His face was a riot of emotions, with anger coming out on top.

"What are you doing here?" he said.

"I don't think you did it," I said.

His mouth opened. Nothing came out.

"Tell me why you think you're here," I said.

"She gave me up! I was with her when that chick was smoked. I never gave her any necklace!"

"What about the DNA?"

He shook his head. "Somebody planted it. Had to."

"That's a hard case to make, Rory."

"I swear I didn't do it. They want to take me down."

"Who does?"

"Donahue! All of them."

"Who's them?"

Rory looked like he was about to spout a geyser of words, but stopped himself. He looked at me a long time.

Finally he said, "How do I know I can trust you?"

"I'm here, right?"

"They could have sent you."

"I don't work for Donahue," I said.

"You work for Jennison."

"I *worked* for him. That job's done."

"He's in on all that, too."

"What exactly is he in on?"

O'Connor leaned closer to the glass, as if that made a difference. In a low voice he said, "Roids. They're trying to make a new juice. Supposed to make you strong and ... what's the word they like? Vicious. Like an animal. And not traceable. So he's gonna make it and sell it for a fortune, to fighters. The military. Only they haven't worked out all the kinks. Like the one that makes you go nuts."

"Tell me about that."

"Random ways. Coming off it, certain guys go crazy."

I thought of Archie losing it when Ira and I first interviewed him.

"It messes with the ladies, too," he said.

"How so?"

Rory gave a little smile. "Makes 'em sexually aggressive. Which ain't all bad. I gave a dose to Derinda once and let me tell you—"

"You don't have to," I said.

"They set me up good, didn't they?" he said.

"Do you have any other way to prove where you were on the night Missy Nolan was murdered?"

"I tell you I was with Derinda the whole time. This is messed up!"

"Life usually is," I said. "But I'll do what I can."

"Why, man? What's in this for you?"

"I helped cause this mess," I said. "And I was taught you should always clean up after yourself."

"That's kind of crazy," he said.

"Isn't it, though?" I said.

I had lunch in Chinatown. Szechuan chicken with orange peel sauce and a Tsingtao beer. The place was old school with a gold dragon on the wall and square tables with linen tablecloths. The lunch crowd was local and one table with three older men was engaged in a spirited discussion in their native tongue.

Outside and across the street you'd think you were back in the 1950s. Chinese street vendors selling homemade zongzi from a cart, others with blankets and mats on the sidewalk holding oranges or bars of soap or knickknacks for the tourists. It was like a time-warp bubble.

How soon before it popped? It was coming. Developers were taking over because of the demand for high-end housing near downtown. Young, urban professionals were moving in like those locusts in *The Good Earth*.

The way of the world, though Chinatown had held its glorious own here. It's actually not the original Chinatown dating from the 1800s. That's buried under Union Station, which razed the buildings when it was built in the 1930s. So the resilient Chinese relocated and who could blame this generation for hanging on to as many of the old ways as possible?

As I was finishing my meal my phone buzzed. The ID was Kaiser, the big HMO. How'd they get my number?

"Yes?" I said.

"Is this Mr. Romeo?" It was a woman's voice, a slight Hispanic accent.

"It is."

"I'm calling from Kaiser Hospital in Panorama City. Do you know a Kathy Nolan?"

"Yes."

"She asked me to call you. Is it possible that you could come and see her?"

"What's wrong?"

"I can only tell you she requested that you come."

I t took me forty-five minutes to get over to the hospital and park. Inside I got a visitor's badge and directions to Kathy Nolan's room

She was bandaged up pretty bad. Her eyes were closed. A nurse was at her bedside and motioned to me to step outside the room.

"You are Mr. Romeo?" she said.

I nodded.

"I called you," she said. She was mid-thirties, medium height. The photo ID clipped to her smock said *Juana Alvarez.*

"What happened?" I said.

"The police are going to come back to question her," Nurse Alvarez said. "She insisted on talking to you."

"Can I?"

"Only for a few minutes, please."

"All right."

I went in and stood by the bed. Half of Kathy Nolan's face was bruised. She had gauze around her head and her right arm. Her left arm had an IV stuck in it.

"Kathy?" I said.

She opened her puffy eyes. Fear and hurt were in them.

"How did this happen?" I said.

Whispering through her cracked lips, Kathy said, "Man."

"A man did this?"

She gave me a small, tortured nod.

"What did he look like?" I said.

"Mask."

"He wore a mask?"

Kathy Nolan gave me the smallest of nods.

"Why did he do this?" I said.

Putting her hand on my arm, she said, "Wanted ..."

"Yes?"

"Missy gave . . . me ... pictures."

Tumblers clicked in my brain. "From that box of photographs I asked you about at Archie's apartment?"

Nod. "Sorry ... Lied."

"Why did Missy give you the pictures?"

"Wanted me ... hide them. I wouldn't ... tell."

"This man beat you up because he wanted you to give him the pictures?"

Nod.

"Did you?" I said.

"No."

"Would you recognize his voice if you heard it again?"

"Maybe ... low ... scary."

"How did Missy get the pictures?" I said.

"Stole."

"From Archie?"

Nod.

"Did she tell you why?"' I said.

"Money," Kathy said. She squeezed my arm.

"Where are the pictures now?"

"Promise."

"Yes?"

"Get them," she said. "Hide them."

"All right."

"Promise."

"I promise," I said. "You're my client now."

She closed her eyes with what looked like relief. "In ... cake box. In ... my freezer."

Clever woman. Not a place your average thug would check for photographs.

"There's ... a key," she said. "Under snail ... in carport ... window box."

"A snail?"

"Cer ... ceramic."

"The ceramic snail in the window box in your carport. You have a house key underneath."

"Be careful," she said.

"You rest easy now," I said.

I didn't want to go to Kathy's house in the daylight, so I drove over to Jimmy Sarducci's gym. I found him looking over a couple of fighters in the ring.

"Think I could take them?" I said.

Jimmy said, "You're smarter, but you're also older."

"Come on, Jimmy. Thirty-five is the new twenty-one."

"Only if you're pumped full of HGH."

"Like Casey Strickland?" I said.

Jimmy shook his head. "I don't like him. He's full of somethin' all right."

"I'm going to fight him," I said.

"Serious?" Jimmy said.

"And I'm going to need somebody in my corner."

I put my hand on Jimmy's shoulder.

Jimmy said, "When's this supposed to happen?"

"I haven't set it up yet, but it'll be soon."

"For Donahue?"

"He'll be part of it," I said.

"Then I want nothin' to do with it."

"Not even for me?"

"Especially not for you. I don't want to see you dirtied."

"Already on me, Jimmy. I thought you and I could do some cleanup together."

He shook his head. "I just want my gym, talk to a few old-timers every now and then, take life easy."

I shrugged. "I understand. Guy gets to be your age, he's entitled to take the easy way out."

"Hey, what?" He pulled himself up to his full, five-three height.

"I get it, Jimmy," I said. "The fight gets too tough, time to sit on the back porch and clip your toenails. Listen to the sound of the grass growing. No need for anything courageous."

"You want I should bust you in the chops?"

"At least that would tell me you've still got some fire," I said.

Jimmy arched his eyebrows then squinted at me. "I know what you're doing. That won't work on me. I don't rattle."

"I wouldn't want to rattle you at this point in your life. That would be cruel. Old men shouldn't be made sport of."

Jimmy made a hissing sound, turned his back on me, walked— no, stomped—over to the far wall. He picked up a medicine ball and came back to me.

"What kind of shape you in?" he said.

"Look at me," I said. "Have you seen anything more magnificent outside of a museum of Greek statuary?"

He shoved the ball in my stomach. I took it with a pronounced *oomph*.

"You're a tomato can," Jimmy said. "If I'm going to do this thing, you're going to start right now and get in shape."

"That's what I'm here for."

"Go get dressed. Then I'm going to put you through Jimmy's special grinder."

It started with five minutes of suicides. That's a special form of wind sprint, going back and forth as fast as you can across the full expanse of the gym floor. I run on the sand and swim in the ocean, but there's a special burn in the lungs that you only get with suicides.

Which Jimmy calls his warm-up exercise.

Then it was five minutes on the heavy bag. No let up. Punches and kicks. By the time I was finished I was flopping sweat and sucking wind. Jimmy tossed me a towel and gave me one minute to rest.

We moved onto burpees. This is usually done with the body only. Dropping down to push-up position, coming back up and finishing with a jump. But Jimmy did it with dumbbells. So down I would go, then back to a squat and then up in the air holding two ten-pound dumbbells in my hands.

"You're off to an okay start," Jimmy said.

After one minute of rest it was on to the jump rope. Five minutes. I was training for five-minute rounds with a one-minute blow in between.

Over to the speed bag next. At the end of five minutes my arms felt like two overweight Russians after a vodka party.

Finally, Jimmy put me in the ring with a sparring partner, a good-looking kid in his early twenties, full of swag and quickness. It was good for me. All my fast-twitch muscles were getting out of their hammocks and prepping for battle.

The kid didn't mess around. Gave me a couple of nice body shots. He didn't have dynamite in his fists, but there was plenty of pop. I concentrated on tattooing his face with jabs.

When I was done and sitting on a stool with a towel wrapped around my shoulders, Jimmy came over and said, "You need to do this four more times this week."

"You sure you weren't a Spanish inquisitor in a past life?" I said.

"A what?"

"Am I free to go?"

"Only if you want to be a tomato can," he said.

"I've been opened up and poured out," I said.

He tweaked my skull. "We need to talk strategy."

After I showered and dressed, I spent an hour in Jimmy's office. He went over everything he knew about Casey Strickland, which wasn't a lot. But he was confident about what he thought the first moves would be.

. . .

On a cot in Jimmy's office I took a blissful ten-minute nap that lasted an hour. When I got up my leg muscles told me to lie back down. I didn't listen, walked out to the gym and saw twilight outside.

Kathy Nolan lived in a rented two-bedroom house in Sunland. Not exactly the garden spot of Los Angeles County. Packed up against the brown, scrubby San Gabriel mountains, the word that comes to mind during the day is *dry*. The streets are cracked and the palm trees look tired.

At night, the cracks are hidden and the hills are black.

I parked on the street around the block. There was a party going on somewhere in the neighborhood. The thudding of a major-league sound system boosted the night, and muffled voices laughed and yakked in some backyard.

At the corner I made like a jogger. I wanted to look like a guy out for a run as I cruised by Kathy's house one time. That gave me a chance to see if anybody was parked and watching the place. I passed the house, kept going to the opposite corner, then crossed the street and ran back up the same way.

No one in any parked cars.

I passed an old man walking a small dog.

The dog yipped and the man said, "Winston!" and the little dog stopped.

There was order in the universe.

Once more I crossed the street. Kathy's house had an open car port. I found the window box which held two dead plants. Between the plants was the ceramic snail. It was about the size of the dog that had yipped at me.

I lifted it and found the key in the dirt.

It opened the door next to the window box, and in I went.

Using my keychain flashlight I found my way to the kitchen and the two-door refrigerator.

I opened the freezer.

On the top shelf, next to a bag of peas, was a pink-and-white cake box. I took out the box and opened it. A square of tin foil took up the whole bottom of the box. I unfolded three sides of the foil, enough to see a collection of photographs inside. I folded them up again, closed the freezer, took the box.

I put the key back under the snail. Then I drove back to the Cove, taking the 101 all the way to Las Virgenes, then cutting through the canyon to PCH.

Once inside my place I used a Kleenex to take each photo by the corner and put them on my coffee table. Seventeen photos in all, 5x7 size. Eight were of Shad Halls. The other photos were also of young men. I separated those photos off to the side as I concentrated on the pictures of Halls.

I recognized him from the distant memory of his murder. A sorority sister I knew at Yale was broken up about it and showed me his picture in the newspaper. A head shot. That same shot showed up every now and then on blogs and internet sites reminiscing about The Hollywood Hunk murder.

Two of the photos had a floral background. Someone's garden, or a park. Halls had his shirt off, showing six-pack abs. He was looking at the camera with a brooding face that was a little too intentional. He had a nice V shape going, from shoulders to waist, where tight blue jeans began.

Another photo showed him mugging for the camera—tongue sticking out, eyes wide. Again, no shirt, the photo taken from mid-torso up. Behind him was a plain wall. No way to tell if this was a studio or living space.

One photo had him with his hair long, dressed in a medieval vest that opened to those abs, and holding a wooden staff with both hands, upraised. This allowed for his left bicep to be shown in all its ripped glory. He looked like a Hercules from the Kevin Sorbo era. I surmised this might have been used by

Halls for a composite layout, what actors used to carry to auditions.

In two of the photos Halls appeared changed. A little older. His face had lost what some poet might have called the springtime of youth. One of these photos, taken in what appeared to be the same spot as the mugging picture, showed Halls shirtless again. But he was thicker, more muscular. And his eyes had changed. From brooding anti-hero to something darker. I could see Shad Halls being cast as the young Hannibal Lecter.

The other photo was a departure from all the others. In this one he was lying face down on a table of some sort. No clothes, full body shot. His head was on a pillow. His expression was dull. Eyes open but with nothing behind them. He could have been drugged. Or dead. Or massively depressed.

The last photo was artistic, a side shot of Halls posing naked in shadow lighting, front leg tastefully forward. Halls was leaning back in the position of an archer, one arm outstretched, the other pulling the invisible bow string. It was Shad Halls as Greek statue. Ideal. Godlike.

Using the tweezers, I turned the photo over. On the back was written, in black, felt-tip, handwritten script—*Sagittarius.*

Latin for archer.

Roman, not Greek.

But who had written the word?

Next to the word *Sagittarius* was a date—6/31/95.

I turned the other photos over. On each of them, with the same felt-tip ink, was a date. The earliest was 2/23/95. That was on the back of one of the brooding-boy photos. The other like photo was dated 3/31/95.

The photo with the latest date was the one of Halls on the table. That was dated 12/24/95.

The photos were a record, but of what? Body image? If these were indeed taken by Archie's father, what was his interest in Halls? Was he the young man's manager? Lover? Pet project? It could have been any of those things.

The only sure thing was that these photos were purposeful, not random. There was a method here.

That brought me to the other photos in the box. Different men, same poses, showing abs. Two shots were in a nicely furnished apartment. Two were outside at a park. The trees in the background were in soft focus, so the photographer knew what he was doing.

And then I stopped cold on three photos of the same guy. He had wild red hair. Not handsome of face, as Shad Halls had been. Eyes kind of close set.

No way.

I fished through a drawer in the kitchen and found a magnifying glass. I went from photo to photo with the glass, and back again. In one photo the kid had a smile, an innocent one, like he was playing a game with a friend.

In the middle photo, the expression was a teenager's idea of brooding and seductive. Squinty eyes and pouty lips.

In the third he was looking up from the floor, where he sat cross-legged, bare-chested in underwear. This was the most natural pose. Expressionless. One might even say lost.

Putting those three together in my mind, and using a little imagination to add twenty years, pounds of muscle, and tattoos, the person I was looking at in those photos was Die Scum himself.

I called Ira. I told him about the pictures and filled him in on everything that had happened, including to Kathy Nolan.

"These were the pictures Archie told me about," I said. "Missy stole them. She was going to try to get money for them. Sell them to a reporter maybe. She was killed over them, and I think I know why."

"Tell me," Ira said.

"I think Archie's father, the Hollywood Hunk murderer, is alive and well and living in Los Angeles."

Ira didn't say anything for a long moment. "You have anything to back that up?"

"Not yet," I said. "I'm working on it."

"How, Michael?"

"I've got some ideas."

"Oh, dear."

"We need to do this right," I said.

"What is your definition of right?"

"We need to clear Rory O'Connor," I said.

"Is he our client now?"

"Pro bono," I said.

"Thank you for telling me," Ira said.

"The lead detective on the Hollywood Hunk murder," I said. "What was his name?"

"Reed," Ira said. "Ted Reed. I had some interaction with him back in the day."

"Is he still around?"

"I can check."

"Do that," I said. "I want to bring him in on this."

It took the great Ira Rosen only forty minutes to get back to me. He'd found retired LAPD detective Ted Reed, who agreed to meet with me the next day at Lake Hollywood Park.

"I want to know what else you're planning, Michael," Ira said.

"I'm not sure myself," I said. "But after it's all over, you'll be the second or third to know about it."

"Who will be the first?"

"Either the cops or the feds," I said.

"Michael!"

Lake Hollywood is not actually a lake. It's a reservoir. But far be it from Hollywood to be wedded to truth.

The park, though, is nice. Tucked up against the scrubby hills, it's a green, grassy place to walk a dog or have a lunch, all under the Hollywood sign. Which was a fitting place to meet with Ted Reed. Up there was where the pieces of Shad Halls were found.

It was around noon. I found Reed sitting on a bench. He had a sack lunch beside him. He was in his mid-sixties, stout around the waist. He had on khaki pants and slip-on tennis shoes, and a short-sleeved white shirt that an accountant or old-school detective might have sported. His thinning gray hair was neatly combed. A cane rested on the end of the bench.

Reed stood up to greet me. We shook hands. Then he lowered himself back on the bench with some effort.

"Everything okay?" I said.

"You know, it's funny," he said. "I survive four years in the Army, four on patrol in South Central, sixteen years of homicide investigation. Not once do I get shot, stabbed, crashed into or spit on. Then I retire and two years later they cut off my leg."

He knocked on his left leg.

"It's the cheapest they got," Reed said. "Insurance company probably picked this up at Costco. You gotta replace 'em every three or four years. That's my future."

"You should be able to get a ten pack at Costco," I said.

Reed laughed. "I'm not bitter, really. I like to come up here and sit and watch people. I spent so many years talking to killers and rapists and people lying for killers and rapists. I just like to soak in the normal."

"That's a good soak," I said.

"You never know what any of those people're doing in the dark," he said. "But at least they look normal. I got to have my fantasy life."

"We've all got that dark side," I said.

That prompted a studious look from Detective Reed. "You got that exactly right," he said. "Most people, you ask 'em, they say they don't. They think they're pretty good."

"We have a great capacity to deceive ourselves."

"You don't talk like a dumb grunt," Reed said.

"I'll take that as a compliment," I said.

Reed reached in his brown bag and pulled out a plastic bag. It had a sandwich in it. White bread, cut on the diagonal. He opened the bag and took out half the sandwich. He held it out to me.

"No, thanks," I said.

"Tuna fish," he said. "I mix up a little mayo and some of that Trader Joe's Everyday Seasoning in it. Ooh-la-la, as the French say."

"Do the French really say that?"

"Heck if I know," Reed said, and took a bite.

"Thanks for seeing me," I said.

"Rosen vouched for you," Reed said. "Otherwise I wouldn't've. Every year they gotta put out some show on the Hollywood Hunk murder." His voice dripped derision when he said *Hollywood Hunk*. "Reporters try to get to me. I just turn 'em down. It's like they come around with a big cup of salt and they want to rub it in the old wound."

"Still a wound?"

"Always will be," he said. "You don't get over the unsolveds. If you've got half a heart, that is. This one took on its own life. It was right after the O.J. trial and the papers needed to keep up circulation. This was it. Shad Halls, this impossibly handsome actor, is cut up in three pieces, his head set on a stone under the Hollywood sign. How could they resist?"

"How long did you work the case?"

"Almost six months," he said. "We thought we had the guy, a porno actor, called himself Woody Wildman."

"I've heard the name."

Reed smiled. "Real name, Schinski. He and Halls had been an item, we discovered from looking into the Halls effects. But Schinski had a stone-cold alibi. He just didn't want to tell us about it at first. Turns out he was shacked up with a producer in a chateau in Vail, Colorado at the time of the murder. He didn't want to name names because he thought it would ruin his career. He had delusion of grandeur, if you'll pardon the expression. He actually thought he could be another Jean-Claude Van Damme."

"Did we need another?" I said.

"Somewhere along the line we were able to convince him that a long-term prison sentence was bad for his career, too. So he gave us the name of the producer, we talk to the producer, and he sweated bullets until he admitted that Schinski had been with him."

"Which left you where?" I said.

"At a pet store," Reed said. "See, I wondered if Halls wasn't done that way to cover up some medical experimentation."

"As in?"

"Halls, he was dubbed the Hollywood Hunk for a reason. The guy was known for his bod, let's face it. He wasn't much of an actor. He made two straight-to-video movies, *Back to Iraq II* and *Mercenary Clones.*"

"I must have missed those," I said.

"You and the entire population of Earth. But here's the interesting thing. A year before he made those, you know where he was? Working in a pet store. And he looked about twenty pounds overweight. I got a picture of the staff of Paws & Claws. He's in there looking all chunk chunk. So what happens? A year later he's ripped and making his first movie."

"It wouldn't be the first time a guy turned his body around."

"Somebody asked him in an interview about it, and he didn't give a very good answer. He mentioned a gym. I checked out the gym. He was never a member there. So I asked a few of his friends what was going on, and one of them, a guy named Samuels, thought Halls was taking some sort of dietary supplement. But Halls told him not to tell anybody."

"Didn't want the secret out."

"At the same time, this friend told me Halls would sometimes act really whacked out. He got into fights on the set for no reason. He once bit a chunk out of a guy's leg." Reed's eyes started to dance in the sunlight. "So here's the theory. He was getting ripped through some drug that messed with his mind. I mean, everybody at the pet store he used to work with said Halls was gentle as a kitten before he transformed. That was back in the early stages of people looking for the fountain of youth. The steroid era in base-ball was getting going. In Hollywood there was a big black market for drugs made over in Europe. Cell therapies, crazy-named drugs. I remember Sylvester Stallone said he injected Gerovital H3 into his butt three times a day. Turned out it was nothing but a topical anesthetic. Stallone would've been better off with Preparation H."

That deserved a smile. I gave him one.

"The feds broke up a big ring in 1992," Reed said. "But that didn't mean the black market went away. They never do. They just change colors. What I think is that Halls got into something, an experimental drug. It gave him a great body but it also messed with his mind. That was the motive. My partner kept insisting it was a sex thing. I think it might have been a drug thing. Maybe Halls was going to talk to the feds. He was gutted to get rid of the biological evidence. Testing in those days wasn't what it is today."

"Why not just get rid of the body?" I said.

"Two theories on that. The killer wanted him found. He wanted Halls to be a warning to others who threatened to talk. Halls was tortured, poor kid. His genitals were scorched."

"Doesn't that point to a sex motive?" I said.

"Or it was set up to look that way," Reed said.

A police chopper came into view in the distance, from the downtown side, heading toward us. We both watched it like it was some monster goose flying north for the summer.

"I'll miss that sound," Detective Reed said.

"Helicopter?" I said.

"It's home."

"Where you going?"

"Oklahoma City," he said. "To be close to my daughter and grandson."

I nodded, waited for more. But that was it. Except for a sad longing in his eyes.

"Now tell me, investigator," Reed said. "Why'd you want to hear all this?"

"You looked at another suspect," I said. "Gavin Jennison."

Reed snapped a look at me. "That was never made public. How do you know that name?"

So I told him the whole story. Retired detective Ted Reed did not take a single bite of his sandwich the whole time. And when I was finished, he stuffed the sandwich in the bag and set it behind him.

"I need those pictures," Reed said.

"I know you do," I said. "And I want you to have them."

"And?"

"I need a little more time."

"Time for what?" Reed said.

"I have to put some things together," I said.

"Is it money you want?"

"No. I want to know about Gavin Jennison."

He studied me for a moment, as if he wasn't sure what to think. Then he said, "We questioned him once. He was a cool customer. Refined, well spoken. He had a wandering eye."

"Wandering?"

"Like that actor, Jack Elam. Do you know about Jack Elam?"

"Name doesn't ring a bell."

"You would know him in a second if you saw his face. He was a popular heavy in westerns in the fifties and sixties. One of his eyes was off. Gave him a sinister look. It was the same with Jennison. We questioned him because he did a lot of business with the pet store where Halls was employed. It wasn't all that strange because the guy was a veterinarian. But we got a statement from one of the other employees that he and Halls seemed to be very chummy. But that was as far as it went. We couldn't find any other corroborating evidence to hold him or question him further. But it wasn't long after our initial questioning that he decided to leave the country."

"Anything else about him? Height, weight?"

"I think he was five-eleven or so, maybe one-seventy. Looked in good shape. He did have a scar on his right palm. That was the only other identifying feature about him. It was raised scarring, a straight line from the base of his index finger to the middle of the palm. He told us it was due to an attempt to save the life of a dog in an emergency situation. I didn't buy it, but what can you do?"

"Maybe you can have another crack at him," I said.

"Huh?"

"What if he's back?" I said.

"You've seen him?"

"Maybe."

He grabbed my arm like it was a lifeline hurled over a ship. "You got to tell me."

"I'm not sure yet," I said. "But I think I can find out."

"Listen," he said. "I want in on this. I want to be the one to bring him in. I need to be the one."

"I know," I said. "And you will be."

The next day I arranged two meetings on the west side. The first was with Archie Jennison at the Venice bar where we'd first met. I made it sound like a bury-the-hatchet thing and in a way, it was. I wanted to bury it in Archie's head far enough that it would jar him into some admissions.

I was there first and sat at the bar, sipping a Smithwick's. Archie arrived with a smile and a pat on my back, just as if nothing had ever gone wrong between us. But it seemed like half of it was an act.

He ordered a Bushmill's Black, neat, and said, "I was glad to hear from you, Mike."

"Yeah?"

"We been through too much to be at odds. All the way back to Nashville, remember?"

"Last time we were on a card."

"That was some night," Archie said. "You won, then I won, and we went out after and closed a couple of bars."

"It was one bar, Arch. And it was still going when we left."

"Those were good days." He lifted his Bushmill's and knocked it back. Then motioned to the bartender to hit him again.

"They were days," I said. "Not all good."

"Come on, we were young bulls, you and me. And the ladies ..."

"The past is only prologue," I said.

He smiled. "There you go again, professor. I'm glad we—"

"I want to run something by you, Arch."

"Sure," he said.

The bartender poured another shot into Archie's glass. Archie raised it then knocked it back. When he put the glass down his expression was troubled. Like he knew something was coming.

"I've got this crazy idea," I said. "You ever get crazy ideas?"

"Too many," Archie said.

"This one is about Rory O'Connor, the Hollywood Hunk murder, and you."

"Me?"

"Let's start with O'Connor."

"It's over, Mike. What're you pressing for?"

"I don't think Rory O'Connor killed Missy," I said.

"Who cares what you think?" His face started to flush. I knew it wasn't from the booze.

I said, "Problem is, somebody used me to nail Rory. I don't like being used."

"What do you got to go over all this?" Archie said.

"That's kind of a funny answer," I said.

"What's funny about it?"

"I would have thought your answer would be, who? Who used you? But you didn't ask me that. It's like you know it's true."

"Come on, Mike. It's over."

"You keep saying that, like you want it to be true."

Archie motioned to the bartender. "I'm gonna have another and leave."

"Casey Strickland killed Missy," I said.

He studied me for a moment. "You got to be kidding."

"I have a witness," I said.

"Who?"

I shook my head.

The bartender gave Archie his shot. Archie took it up immediately.

"There's more," I said. "Somebody beat up Kathy Nolan, pretty bad."

Archie looked at his glass. "Kathy?"

"She's in the hospital," I said.

"How bad?"

"Don't you know?"

Archie finished his drink and slammed the glass on the bartop. "What are you tryin' to say?"

"I'm trying to figure out who would want to beat her in order to find those photos," I said. "You know what I'm talking about. Did you beat her up?"

"Come on, Mike."

"Answer me."

"No! Okay?" He started to raise his arm for the bartender. I caught it and pushed it down.

"Then you know who did," I said.

"No."

"I can keep digging, Archie."

He yanked his arm away, spun on the barstool to face me head on. "Leave it alone, Mike, I'm tellin' you."

"Why don't you tell your father?"

That froze him up nice and tight.

"What's Donahue got to do with all this?" I said.

Archie got off the stool. "Why couldn't you just go away? What is it with you?"

"I don't like being played," I said. "I get kind of annoyed when I am."

"Stay out of it," he said. He turned and walked out.

M y second meeting was in Westwood. I parked in the lot on Broxton and got a little exercise walking over to the federal building on Wilshire. I went through the scanner and then to the security desk. I gave them my name and said I wanted to see Agent Holly Samara. No, I did not have an appointment, but did have an invitation. What I didn't tell them was that last time I'd seen Agent Samara she said she'd like to buy me a drink sometime. That time, I decided, was now.

I was told to have a seat on a bench.

A few minutes later, Agent Holly Samara exited an elevator and walked over to me. I stood to greet her.

"Mike Romeo," she said. "It's been too long."

Her handshake was as crisp as handcuffs closing. She was dressed in a blue suit over a black blouse. Without the security credential around her neck, she might have passed for the publisher of a fashion magazine or the star of a new reality series about federal law enforcement agents.

"What brings you to the west side?" she said.

"I'm looking for some inside information," I said.

"Then that means come inside."

We took the elevator up to the seventeenth floor and got buzzed through to the offices. This was an FBI field office, and Holly Samara was on assignment here as a DEA liaison.

Which meant a small but efficient work space.

She sat behind her desk. It had a computer monitor and a small plant on it.

I took the chair opposite her desk.

"What kind of information are you looking for?" Holly Samara asked.

"Similar to the biomedicals you were tracking last time," I said. "I wanted to know if you were still on that."

"I can give you a qualified yes."

"How about over-qualified?"

"Can't go any further on that."

"What about synthetic steroids specifically related to athletic abilities? Strength, speed, that sort of thing?"

"That's happening all over. As long as the juice is not illegally moved or sold, it's not under our purview. It's up to the governing bodies of the sport to regulate."

"So you're not aware of trafficking in illegal 'roids around town?"

"I can give you a no on that one. I'm not saying it doesn't happen, but it hasn't reached a level to register with us. Why? Do you know something?"

"I can give you a qualified yes," I said.

"You continue to intrigue me," she said, leaning back in her chair.

I said, "Coming from a federal agent, that's disconcerting."

"That's just it. You use words like *disconcerting*."

"It just popped out."

"No, you're highly educated. But you look like a boxer. And I think you're not a stranger to trouble."

"May I ask where this is going?" I said.

"As I recall, last time you were here I said I'd buy you a drink."

"I recall that, too."

"The offer is still open."

"The offer," I said, "is accepted."

"There's a place in the Village called Lex. How about we meet there in an hour?"

"I'd like to mix pleasure with business," I said.

"Fine," she said. "How much of each will be entirely up to you."

I walked back to Westwood Village and strolled around, looking at the UCLA students and well-heeled shoppers as they avoided the homeless on the corners and, largely, each other.

Since I had some time to wrestle with—I don't like killing time, just making it sweat a little—I went onto the UCLA campus. Always interesting to see what the kids are into these days.

The first poster I saw publicized a meeting to "explore romantic and platonic relationships by way of group discussion and the dance." I assumed *the dance* was generic for free-form body movement and not the studied intricacies of the Lindy Hop. At least that's what the accompanying photo seemed to indicate, showing several students in poses that looked like auditions for a new version of *The Karate Kid*.

Inside a building called Ackerman I spied a vending machine and thought I might snag a Snickers. On closer inspection, though, I saw it was a machine that dispensed condoms, pregnancy tests, and a variety of school supplies like pens and note cards. Interesting mix, that.

On the wall next to the vending machine was a poster with a pink background, with the following script: **KEEP CALM and CARRY cONdoms**.

I'm not sure the London citizens during the blitz would have appreciated that. From bravery in war to the sanitizing of recreational sex. Ah, the arc of history.

I was glad it was time to leave this place and meet Agent Holly Samara.

L ex was a nicely appointed restaurant slash bar on Le Conte. A white marble look, like ancient Rome. Julius Caesar would have been at home walking in, raising two fingers and saying, "I'll have five beers."

I took one of the high tables in the bar area. Agent Samara came in about two minutes later. I stood up to greet her. She hung her purse on the chair opposite me, then sat.

"This okay with you?" she said.

"The bar or the company?" I said.

"Both."

"Definitely okay," I said.

A waiter with a top-knot man bun and a five-day stubble of beard carefully manicured to look like unmanicured two-day stubble, asked what we'd like to drink. Agent Samara ordered a Grey Goose martini. I ordered a Corona.

I said, "How'd you get into law enforcement?"

"My grandfather was a police officer here in L.A.," she said. "I was very close to him."

"He's gone now?"

She nodded. "He used to tell me stories about Mickey Cohen and Chief Parker and Jack Webb, you know, *Dragnet.* Jack Webb used to do ride alongs with my grandfather."

"So you got caught up in the romance of it?"

"I wouldn't say romance. I'd say the possibilities. I'm kind of a law-and-order type. Always have been."

"Good thing," I said. "If you're going to be enforcing the laws."

"So," she said. "Business and pleasure. Which shall we take on first?"

"You know how to get right to it," I said.

"Training," she said.

"Let's do business," I said.

"You have the ball," she said.

"There are a couple of loan sharks I want to put out of business."

Raising her eyebrows, she said, "Gambling problem?"

"It's for a friend."

"Uh-huh."

"No, really. This time it's legit. A kid I'm trying to help out."

"Is this drug related?" she said.

"Thankfully, no. It's stupidity related."

"It usually is," she said.

"Doesn't RICO cover loan sharking?"

"That'd be FBI jurisdiction."

"Who you're working with, yes?"

"We'd need a connection to interstate commerce."

"Like somebody doing business that crosses state lines."

"Exactly. In the loan sharking context, it usually means there's a default, and the shark says to the business owner, you have a choice. You can die, or you can give me control of your business. Sure, you can still run it, that's a good front, but the profit goes to me. So choose, loser, what'll it be?"

The server returned with our drinks. We hoisted and clicked and drank. Pleasure making nice inroads on business.

I said, "So that would be enough to give the feds jurisdiction?"

She nodded. "Then it's a matter of priorities. How big is this enterprise?"

"Not very. It's kind of a punk rock band."

For a moment I thought Agent Samar might spit-take her martini. Then she smiled. "Seriously?"

"I don't know if it's neo-punk or ska-punk or—"

"No," she said. "You're wanting me to consider jurisdiction on a shark loan to a band?"

"Not just any band," I said. "Unopened Cheese."

Agent Samara just stared at me.

"Big things waiting to happen?" I said.

"Have they made any money?"

"I'm sure they've made some," I said, then added, "Actually, not so sure."

She shook her head and smiled. "How much was the loan?"

"Originally fifteen thousand," I said.

"That'd be a tough sell in our office," she said.

"What if I could hand them over on the proverbial silver platter," I said.

"There you go again," she said, "using words like proverbial."

"It's a better word than abstruse."

She laughed.

I said, "And of course if you searched their office and seized their computers and phones, you'd find a lot of good stuff."

"If we weren't to get involved," she said, "what would you do?"

"Probably take care of matters myself."

"That sounds awfully close to the line."

"What line?" I said.

"Between criminal behavior and lawful behavior."

"A citizen's arrest is on the right side of the line," I said.

"My advice," she said, "don't try."

"I've been avoiding advice for a good ten years now."

"And what's that gotten you?"

"A free drink," I said, and toasted her with my beer.

"I'm beginning to like you," she said.

"I can use a friend in law enforcement," I said.

"Is that all you want?" she said.

"This is moving kind of fast," I said.

"My schedule doesn't permit any wasted time," Agent Samara said.

"I feel like I should consult an attorney."

She smiled. "Certainly under Miranda you have that right."

"Agent Samara, I—"

"Holly."

"I'm not exactly ... moving in the personal realm right now."

She leaned back in her chair. "Is that a variation of 'It's not you, it's me?' "

"No. It is you. And me. I mean, I'm sort of, what's the word I'm looking for?"

"Disconcerted?"

"That would be a good word," I said.

"Involved with someone else?"

"Not really."

"That's ambiguous."

"It's one of my best features," I said.

"Meaning?"

"If I told you, it wouldn't be ambiguous," I said.

Agent Holly Samara took a sip of her drink. "Now I'm starting to get annoyed."

"I have that effect," I said. "Instead of ambiguous, let's leave it open ended. How's that?"

"Better, I guess."

"I'm working on something," I said. "Call it a personal project. I think I can have it wrapped up in a week or two. Part of it has to do with the loan sharks."

"What about the other parts?"

"Can't go any further than that," I said.

"You're insufferable," she said.

"That's a good word, too," I said.

W e parted with a handshake. She held it longer than average and looked me in the eye. "I don't want to be reading about you in any crime scene report," she said.

"You agents say the sweetest things," I said.

"Wait till you get me alone," she said, and walked off to her car.

I felt good then, good enough to make the call I'd been putting off.

To Zane Donahue's private number.

A voice answered. "Yes?"

"Mike Romeo calling for Mr. Donahue."

"Hold on."

A moment later Donahue said, "Hey, Mike. Ready to talk?"

"As a matter of fact," I said.

"Good! Let's make it tomorrow morning. Marina Del Rey. I want you to see my boat."

A s I turned on Wilshire I noticed I'd picked up a tail. I hate when that happens.

This one was a black car of some kind, two heads that I could see. The driver was wearing shades. How inconspicuous. I almost felt like stopping so I could give him some pointers on how not to be spotted when you're following a car. As in, don't look like a bad guy. Look like a CPA on the way to the office. This guy was an affront to all the people who knew how to do it right.

I kept my speed steady, not wanting to alert him. I had a couple of options.

I could pull a few moves to put some cars, and maybe a truck, in between us. Once out of the sight line I could maneuver to make a quick turn at a light. The point would be to get to the freeway.

My other option was to make my way to the Beverly Hills police station on Rexford and park in front and wait. But that's a move for a good citizen trying to shake a road rager. Road ragers were scared of cops. These guys wouldn't be. They could wait me out. It was their job. I could roust a cop and have him accompany me to the tailing car.

Then I thought maybe they stuck a GPS tracker somewhere under Spinoza. Annoying. It would take an inspection, and probably a sweeper, to find it.

I considered pulling what Joey Feint used to call a Buford. Named for the Union cavalry officer John Buford, who held the high ground at Gettysburg on the first day of the battle. A Buford means you find a favorable position for a direct confrontation. But that worked best when you had a weapon, because maybe the other guys were armed.

That's when I hit a red light. There was a car in front of me. The tailing car was directly behind. I took off my seat belt. If one of the guys got out with a weapon, I had to be ready to jump out and do what my fight-or-flight instinct told me.

The shadows stayed put.

The light changed and on we flowed.

To the next light. This part of Beverly Hills has lights every block and if the traffic or timing's off, you're pumping the brakes a lot. You're watching the agents and lawyers and billionaire wives crossing the street with that anxious look of the perpetually stressed, mixed in with the hipster sales clerks and young dental hygienists all glued to their phones and developing an anxious look of their very own. And then you see—

—a Beverly Hills cop. On a motorcycle. Pulling up in the lane next to you as you wait for the light to change.

Timing is everything in L.A.

I tapped my horn and the helmeted cop turned my way.

"Can we talk?" I shouted, and pointed toward the side.

He made a palms-up gesture.

"Trouble," I said.

He paused, then gave me a quick nod.

The light turned green.

The cop motioned for me to fall in behind him. Two cars went by me in the other lane before I could.

My tail didn't make the lane change.

The cop turned right on a street called Swall. There was a red brick building on the corner. I followed the cop, who turned right into an alley between the building and a residence with a Spanish-tile roof.

He stopped, got off his bike.

I stopped, got out of Spinoza, looking behind to see if my friends were driving by.

They weren't.

"What seems to be the problem?" the officer said.

I went for the official look, took out my wallet and got an Ira lawyer card. "I'm an investigator. I was being followed back there and you came along at just the right time."

He took the card, looked at it. "You kidding?"

"I'm as serious as a plastic surgeon on Rodeo Drive."

The cop did not smile.

"What kind of a car was it?" he said.

"Black Town Car," I said.

"Did you get the license plate?"

"I did, but I suspect it's a phony."

The cop said, "How do you know you were being followed?"

"Experience," I said.

The cop tapped the card on his thumb, looking unconvinced. "Why do you think you're being followed?"

"Good question," I said. "I wish I could ask them."

"Well," the cop said, "maybe you can."

He was looking over my shoulder.

I turned.

And saw the Town Car pulling up behind Spinoza.

"Let's both ask them," I said.

"Let's," the cop said.

. . .

The guy who got out of the back of the Town Car looked like, well, a CPA on the way to the office. Dark blue suit and tie, glasses, on the thin side. Dark hair neatly combed and a pleasant smile. He walked right over to me and the cop.

"Good afternoon," he said.

"Are you following this gentleman?" the cop said.

"Yes, I am," the guy said.

"And why is that?" the cop said.

"I represent someone who is interested in speaking with Mr. Romeo."

He knew me. I didn't know him. That annoyed me.

"No law broken, I trust," the guy said.

"As long as you don't run any red lights," the cop said, and got on his bike.

"I don't want to talk to this guy," I said.

"I think you do," the guy said.

"That's between you two," the cop said. He started up the bike and drove off.

"What's this about?" I said to the guy.

"As I said, I have a client who would like a few words with you."

"Who?"

"I'm not at liberty to say."

"Well then, you're at liberty to get lost."

"I don't believe you want that, Mr. Romeo of Paradise Cove."

"All right, you've done your homework. Who are you?"

"Call me Carl." He put out his hand.

I didn't take it. "Why should I call you at all?"

Carl smiled as he lowered his hand. "It's my client you need to talk to. I don't think it will take too long, but it's definitely important."

"No," I said.

"My client is at the Beverly Wilshire. Everything is above board."

"Have a good day."

I opened Spinoza's door.

"The police in New Haven might be interested in your whereabouts," Carl said.

I closed Spinoza's door.

"Please," Carl said. "Just a few minutes of your time."

"Who's going to pay for parking?"

Carl took out a wallet and handed me a picture of Andrew Jackson.

"For the valet," he said.

I met Carl in the lobby. The guy with the shades who'd been driving the Town Car was waiting for us by the elevators. He was the silent type. He stayed true to form as we took the elevator to the tenth floor.

"How's your day been?" Carl said.

"Are you kidding?" I said.

"I'm from Missouri, originally," Carl said. "We don't kid."

"Then I'm just having a crackerjack day," I said. "Let's catch a movie after this."

The guy with the shades made a noise. It could have been a grunt or a stifled burp.

My day was looking better than ever.

On the tenth floor we walked the plush corridor to a room near the end. Carl held up a key card and the door clicked.

We went in.

The suite was exactly what you'd expect on the tenth floor of the Beverly Wilshire Hotel. Everything looked like it came off a showroom floor yesterday. A vase with red roses rested on top of a glass coffee table as if waiting for a couple to clink champagne glasses. On the wall above the sofa was a framed print of geometric art or artful geometry. I couldn't tell which.

Across the room a glass door looked upon a balcony. Gazing out the door, back to us, was a tall man in a suit. He had gray hair.

He turned around.

It was Mr. Eye Patch.

"**F**inally we meet," he said.

"You've been keeping an eye on me," I said. "Pardon the expression."

"Have a seat," he said.

"I'm not staying long," I said.

"That has yet to be determined," Eye Patch said.

"I'll give you five minutes," I said.

"Please sit," Eye Patch said.

"No, thanks."

The man looked behind me and nodded. I turned around and saw the driver holding a pistol in ready position. He was smiling.

"That's not cricket," I said.

"Sit down, please," Eye Patch said.

"My doctor says I'm not allowed to sit in the presence of guns."

"Sit," Eye Patch said. "Or would you like a bullet to the knee?"

"I'll sit," I said. "But my congressman is going to hear about this."

"I sincerely doubt that."

I sat on the chair that faced Eye Patch.

"I want you to consider this as a court of law," Eye Patch said.

"And you're the judge?" I said.

"So be very careful what you say to me."

"How about a bathroom break?" I said. "Or a sandwich?"

"If I decide you need to be struck on the head, I will give the word. What you say had better satisfy me."

I folded my arms and waited.

Eye Patch said, "You call yourself Mike Romeo?"

I bobbed my eyebrows, Groucho style.

"Verbalize your answers," he said.

"*Sí.*"

Eye Patch nodded at the driver. Before I could turn I got a

clang to the back of my head. With metal. Sparks went off behind my eyes.

"Do you want more of the same?" Eye Patch said.

I rubbed the spot and waited for the ringing in my head to die down.

"Well?" Eye Patch said.

"Romeo," I said. "No secret."

"When did you adopt that name?" Eye Patch said.

"I was born with it," I said.

"I don't think so."

"Then why did you ask?"

"Would you like another blow to the head?"

"You're going to kill me anyway, so have at it."

"Who said anything about killing?"

"It doesn't take a genius," I said.

"I'd rather we put it another way," he said. "You have a chance to get out of here in one piece. But it will require complete truthfulness."

"And trust?"

"Of course."

"Then how about you answer me a question?" I said.

"Maybe."

"Do you have a scar on your right hand?"

A major scowl took over his face. But it was more confusion than anger. If this was Archie's long-lost father, and the Hollywood Hunk killer, he was a good actor, too.

"What an odd question," he said.

"I have a reason," I said.

"The answer is no," Eye Patch said. He put his hand palm up. "Anything else?"

Okay, strike down my big theory. Who else could this guy be?

"I took the name Romeo some time ago," I said. "I didn't want my old name."

"Which was?"

"I'd rather not say."

"I'd rather you did," he said.

"That leaves us with a bit of a conundrum," I said.

"Which can be solved with another tap to the head."

"If that happens, I'll make you kill me," I said. "I'll take whatever flesh I can with me, too."

"You want to die?"

"I'm neutral on the subject."

Behind me, the driver said, "Want me to?"

Carl said, "That wouldn't be advisable."

I started to like Carl.

Eye Patch raised his hand and shook his head. "I want information. I'm going to get it from you one way or another. Believe that much at least."

"You're looking for something," I said. "Why don't you just tell me what it is?"

Eye Patch paused, then reached for a briefcase next to the coffee table. He opened it, took out a single sheet, and handed it to me.

It was a photograph.

Of me when I was fourteen years old.

Rotund, confused Michael Chamberlain, in a prep school photo. No smile on that face. Only eyes that seemed to look through the camera at the uncertain future and trying to keep from folding up into a butter ball.

But how did this guy get this picture?

More to the point, why?

Eye Patch said, "Is that you?"

"Do I look fat to you?" I said.

"Answer the question."

"You know the answer," I said.

"That's the first honest thing you've said to me," Eye Patch said.

"The second," I said. "I really don't care if I die now or later."

"I believe you in that," Eye Patch said. "The jury is still out on whether it will happen."

"Do you want to tell me why that is?" I said.

"I'll get to that."

"Well hurry it up, will you?"

The driver said, "Let me hit him again."

I got ready. If I saw Eye Patch give a nod I was going to helicopter spin out of the chair, cut the guy's legs out from under him and take my chances from there.

But Eye Patch crossed me up.

"Wait outside," he said to his boys.

"Not a good idea," Carl said.

In a calm, controlled voice, Eye Patch said, "Do as I tell you."

I heard a grunt, probably the driver, and then a door open and close.

"I hope this helps with the trust factor," Eye Patch said.

"It's a lot better than clonking me with a gun," I said. "What's with the hard guy routine?"

"You are Michael Chamberlain, correct?"

"I *was* Michael Chamberlain."

"Your parents were killed in that shooting at Yale."

"Obviously."

"After which you disappeared."

"Pretty much."

"To reappear as Mike Romeo, a professional cage fighter."

"For awhile."

Eye Patch nodded. "Now, the Yale killer was a medical student named Benjamin Weeden Blackpoole. The death count was seventeen. Then he shot himself."

That's when it began to dawn on me. "You saw the story on the internet, that Michael Chamberlain may be in Los Angeles."

"That's exactly right," Eye Patch said.

Shortly after I arrived in L.A., to take up residence with Ira Rosen, I got recognized on the street. It was a guy named Jason Pratt, who I knew back in New Haven. We'd been in prep together. He was a little older, and a bully. Later he caught up with me at Yale, tried to bully me again, this time verbally. He was no match for me in that department. I laughed at him, insulted him in Latin and by way of Shakespeare—"Thine face is not worth sunburning." Some girls nearby heard that and laughed. Pratt didn't like that one bit.

When he saw me in L.A. he knew that the New Haven police had been looking for Michael Chamberlain, for reasons that will soon be clear. And when I didn't give him money he spilled the story to a popular crime blog. They hit the net with the headline *Is Michael Chamberlain in Los Angeles?*

"So now what?" I said.

Eye Patch said, "A couple of years after the killings, a man named Thurber McDaniels was murdered in New Haven. That crime has never been solved. I have determined to solve it."

"Why you?" I said.

"Because Thurber McDaniels was my son."

"So you found me," I said.

"I had to," McDaniels said.

"How'd you get involved with Zane Donahue?"

"He's a businessman, just like I am."

"You wanted to find somebody in L.A., not in a legit way, so you somehow found Donahue. He doesn't do anything except for money, so you must have paid him some pretty good green. Enough to get a couple guys with guns to follow me around."

"I want to know what happened," he said. "I need to know ..." His voice trailed off. He looked at the floor. Took a deep breath, and continued. "It is important to me for many reasons."

"Justice?" I said.

"Only partly."

"What's the other part?"

"Peace, I suppose you'd call it. I lost my son twice. The second time was his death. The first time it was something else. I have to know what you know about it."

"Why do you think I know anything about your son?"

His face took on a steely look then. "Facts. Your father was my son's professor at Yale. He had my son expelled for plagiarism. That connects you to my son."

"Flimsy."

"Something tells me it's not."

I tried to read the man's face. There's a tell about grieving. The face fights against the emotion. The forehead tenses, the mouth turns downward. The eyebrows tend to tremble. If it's old grief, as it was here, the signs are subtle.

McDaniels needed it.

"May I know your first name?" I said.

"John," he said.

I nodded. "How well did you know your son after his expulsion?"

John McDaniels sighed. "We were estranged for a time. I was severely disappointed in him, and let him know that. His answer was to withdraw from me. He grew somewhat hard."

"Philosophy," I said.

John McDaniels looked at me, quizzically.

"Philosophy has consequences," I said. "The basic beliefs you adopt have tentacles that go out into every aspect of your life. The sad thing is people aren't really trained to think that way anymore. Your son was a philosophy major. He knew and embraced his philosophy."

"What philosophy?"

"When I was doing my own investigation, I found out that your son was into an ancient Chinese philosopher named Yang Chu. In fact, it was a monograph on Yang Chu that your son copied, verbatim, and turned in to my father, and that got him expelled. Yang Chu did not believe in an afterlife, so anything we do, even evil acts or omissions, which bring us pleasure, are permissible."

For a long moment John McDaniels was silent. Finally, he said, "You send your son to the finest college in America, and this is what you end up with."

"The evidence suggests your son added Hitler to the mix, and started drawing some students around, using drugs as bait. Then culted them."

"What do you mean?"

"I think you know. He turned Benjamin Blackpoole into an acolyte. More than that, he turned Blackpoole into a mass shooter who would go after my father and whoever else was in the way. My mother and fifteen students were in the way that day."

John McDaniels opened his mouth. But nothing came out.

I started to say something but he put up his hand, turned his head away. He walked to the corner of the room. He stood there, back to me, head down. Without turning around he said, "How do you know all this?"

I spoke softly. "When I confronted your son with what I'd figured out, he didn't deny it. Instead, he tried to kill me."

McDaniels turned around. "How?"

"With a samurai sword."

"He had the sword?"

I nodded. "I got under it and gave him a blow to the temple. He fell and hit his head on the corner of a table."

"But he was …"

"Yeah, almost cut in two by the sword. That was me."

McDaniels came back slowly to his chair, sat and laced his fingers together under his chin. "You're saying my son attacked you with that sword?"

"That's right," I said.

"That would make it … self-defense."

"Only if he died from my hitting him, or when he hit the table. Or was in the process of dying. But it's also possible he might have survived both. He wouldn't have survived the sword."

"That would have been …"

"Murder? If I had to plead my case, it would have been some

form of manslaughter. Or a defense like heat of passion. My mind was pretty much on fire when it all went down."

"But either way it was you who killed my son."

"Yes," I said.

He paused. "I thank you for your honesty."

"You wanted trust? You got trust. Now the question is, what are you going to do about it?"

"The New Haven police want to question you."

"I'm well aware."

"I can hold you indefinitely."

"Maybe," I said.

"Maybe?"

"People have tried that before," I said.

He nodded. "I believe your account. I've looked into many eyes in my time, and in my line of business you have to be able to size people up in a hurry."

"What business is that?"

"I'd prefer not to say."

"Trust me," I said.

That got a smile out of him. The first.

He said, "Let's just say it has to do with international sales."

"Weapons?" I said.

"You're very astute," McDaniels said.

"I've been called worse."

He went to the glass door and spoke with his back to me. "I knew my son was troubled, but not to the extent you've explained it. If you were to be questioned, or go on trial, it would all come out, wouldn't it?"

"I don't see how it couldn't," I said.

He didn't move or say anything for a long time. I looked at the roses on the coffee table.

Finally, he turned around and said, "I told you this was like a court of law. And you told me I was the judge. I'm not qualified for that, and don't wish to be. I wish my son to rest in peace. He didn't have that in life and he didn't have it with me. Maybe he can have it now. I can do that much for him. For that much, at least, I thank you."

I stood. "For what it's worth, I'm sorry."

"You lost your parents," he said. "I understand the pain you must have felt."

"Feel," I said.

He nodded. And stuck out his hand. I shook it.

He walked to the door and opened it, letting Carl and the driver back in.

"Gentlemen," he said, "our business is concluded. I will pay you your balance in cash."

As I walked out the driver said, "No hard feelings."

"*Manducare mea bracis*," I said.

Poor guy. He'd be forever wondering what I said to him in Latin. He'd never know I said, "Eat my shorts."

Marina Del Rey is between Venice and Los Angeles International Airport. It's where a lot of rich people park their boats. I got there just before ten in the morning. As I'd been instructed, I drove down a street called Bora Bora Way which terminated at the inlet of the small-craft harbor. In front of me was anything but a small craft. It was Zane Donahue's yacht, *The Max Baer*. He called it that because he owned the house that had long ago belonged to the heavyweight champion.

A woman in white slacks and navy-blue blazer approached my car.

"Mr. Romeo?" she said. She could have been the hostess at a high-end restaurant in Beverly Hills. Or one of the stars of a new TV series called *Donahue's Angels*.

"Here to see Mr. Donahue," I said.

She smiled and handed me a pass to put on Spinoza's dash, then pointed me to a parking spot near the water's edge.

Then she escorted me on board. I felt underdressed in my Hawaiian shirt, jeans and flip-flops. She led me to a deck at the back—er, aft—of the yacht. There at a round table with a white tablecloth sat Zane Donahue. He wore blue shorts with a white belt and a white cotton shirt without a wrinkle. And slip-on loafers with no socks.

But the sun was shining and the sky was blue and the heron skimming the inlet seemed happy enough.

"Welcome aboard," he said. He stood and shook my hand, offered me a chair. He opened a wooden cigar box that was on the table and offered me one. I shook my head.

"I insist," Donahue said. "These are Cuban. *Flor De Cano Diademas.* You have to be pretty big in the commie party over there even to get one of these."

"Or a capitalist with some black market connections," I said.

"I admit nothing but a bias for pleasure," he said. "Please."

I selected one of the sticks and Donahue handed me a silver cutter. I snipped the end. Donahue fired up a lighter and I brought my Cuban to life. He did the same with his.

"Now we can have a civilized talk," he said. "What do you think of my boat?"

"Cleopatra's barge had nothing on this," I said.

"Two-hundred and forty feet of absolute luxury. Twin Caterpillar 2500 horsepower engines. Can get up to eighteen knots. Got my suite on the main deck with terrace and balcony on port and starboard. Even got a library that converts into a movie theater."

"All the comforts of a small city," I said.

"But what I'm proudest of is the cage. A little smaller than what you're used to, but makes for a real intimate gathering, in the cage and out of it."

"This setup must have set you back some," I said.

"I never think in those terms," Zane Donahue said. "Only moving ahead."

The woman in the blue blazer came back carrying a tray with a coffee service and set it on the table.

"May I?" she said to me.

"You may," I said.

She poured a coffee for me.

"Cream or sugar?" she said.

"Nothing," I said.

She poured a cup for Donahue. He took it black, too.

"Thank you, Kami," Donahue said.

Kami smiled at me.

I smiled at Kami.

Donahue smiled at both of us.

And then Kami left.

Talk about being softened up. But I wasn't feeling soft.

"Nice of you to put McDaniels on my tail," I said.

"Ah, I knew it would get back to you. Business is business."

"He paid you well."

"But I want you to know it's not personal," Donahue said.

Of its own accord a snort issued from my nose.

"Now," Donahue said. "You have a proposition for me. Please tell me it includes a fight."

"It includes a fight."

"Superb."

"You also want me on your payroll," I said.

"I do indeed," he said. "And you know I can pay more than you'll get any place else."

"I propose we split the difference," I said. "I will fight for you, but only if certain conditions are met."

He took a long, languid pull on his cigar. Through the gauze of smoke he squinted at me. "You're giving me conditions?"

"This is, after all, a business meeting," I said.

"What if I say my terms, take it or leave it?" Donahue said.

"Then I will finish my cigar, and leave."

He waited a few beats before answering. "I believe you would. Continue."

"I don't want to handle any cash," I said.

"You have to win it first," he said.

"I'll win it," I said.

"I like that about you," he said.

"I'm a likable guy."

"So what about the money?" he said.

"You donate the entire purse, anonymously, to a certain medical clinic."

He studied me for a long moment. "You're not interested in the money?"

"I'm very interested," I said, "in where it goes."

"You some kind of monk or something?" he said. "You think money is the root of all evil?"

"Actually," I said, "it's the love of money that's the root of all evil."

"Money is what got me this yacht," he said. "And these cigars. And I'm still a very nice guy."

I kept myself from snorting. "In addition to that donation, you will make a monthly contribution of five thousand dollars in perpetuity."

Donahue put his head back and laughed. "Right. And why should I even consider for one microsecond doing that?"

"Because it's in your best interest."

"You're going to have to explain that."

"Five grand a month is not that much considering what you're into, what you bring in. Think of it kind of like protection money."

"Protection?"

"Yeah, like in the old days. Neighborhood shop would pay a local black hand thug a certain amount to keep the cops away and to keep his shop from being burned down at night. Protection."

Leaning forward, Zane Donahue pointed at me with his cigar. "You think I need protection?"

"I'm talking about exchange here that will benefit you and mankind. How often you get a deal like that offered to you?"

"Let's be clear about something," Donahue said. "I like you. I think you know that. But this isn't junior high school. This isn't you come over to my house and spend the night and we'll play video games. You don't want to get too cute with me. If I was in some movie from the nineteen-forties, I'd say, do you know who you're dealing with?"

"And I throw it back at you. Do you know who you are dealing with?"

"I know exactly," he said. "It's in my interest to know."

"I don't think you do," I said. "You see, I'm the gingerbread man."

That put a puzzled look on his face. He was waiting for me to explain. I let him wait. He took a sip of coffee. That was long enough.

"It's a children's story," I said. "A story my mom read to me when I was little. From a great old book with colorful pictures. It's the story of a little old man and a little old woman and they didn't have kids. One day the old lady says, I'm going to make a gingerbread boy. So she rolled out the gingerbread and cut it into the shape of a boy. Gave him eyes made out of raisins and a little hat made out of white frosting."

"Does this story have a point?" Donahue said.

"Absolutely," I said. "But you've got to appreciate the context. So the old lady puts the gingerbread boy in the oven and forgets about him. When she figures out the little guy is burning, she opens the oven door and the gingerbread boy jumps out and starts running out of the house."

"How does he do that? I thought he was a cookie."

"Children's story, Zane. Go with it."

"I don't know why, but go ahead."

"So the old man and old lady go running after him, and he looks back at them and laughs and he starts singing, 'Run, run, run. Catch me if you can. You can't get me, I'm the Gingerbread Man."

"I like his attitude."

"So he keeps on running, and a cow, and a horse, a farmer with a pitchfork, they all want to eat him. And he keeps running away and giving them that same song. And then he gets to a river. Which is a problem for a cookie. He can't get wet."

"Makes sense," Donahue said. "We almost done?"

"There's a fox who shows up and says, Jump on my tail and I'll take you across. As the water gets deeper the gingerbread man has to get on the fox's back. A little further and deeper and he has to get on the fox's shoulder. And then his nose. The fox gets to the other side, leans his head back, and chomps up the gingerbread man."

"And?"

"That's the end of the story."

Zane Donahue frowned. "You told me this why?"

"Because I'm the gingerbread man. You can't catch me."

"What if I'm the fox?"

"Here's where my story is a little different. I'm a different kind of gingerbread man. I can kick you in the teeth. If you try to gobble me up, and miss, you might very well become a fox fur. There's a certain amount of trouble that you, as a businessman, don't want."

"I've been dealing with trouble all my life," Donahue said.

"Not the gingerbread kind. The kind that gathers information about illegal steroids, human experimentation, both of which violate federal law. Information like that could eventually get to the Department of Justice, the FBI, and the Drug Enforcement Agency. Not to mention all the big news outlets. In fact, if anything should happen to the gingerbread man, all that information will be released."

Donahue put his cigar in his mouth and left it there. He laced his fingers over his stomach. "You're bluffing."

I put my cigar in my mouth and laced my own fingers over my stomach.

And waited.

"It's a good bluff," Donahue said.

He put out his hand. I shook it.

· · ·

I spent the next week working on my wind—sprinting in the sand, swimming in the ocean. Went a couple hours a day to Jimmy Sarducci's gym. Heavy bag, speed bag, jump rope, spar.

In the evenings I gave my mind a Spartan bath. There is a story about the Spartan philosopher Chilon the Wise, who was once called to speak to the warriors about to go into battle in the Peloponessos. He said only one thing, "See the victory." When a soldier asked Chilon what he meant, Chilon stepped up to him and said, "I see myself rebuking you." And then he slapped him.

With that, he withdrew from the assembly.

In my daydreams I saw Die Scum, and slapped him repeatedly.

And then, on Thursday, I went and saw personally another guy who needed to be slapped.

"Money," I said through the glass door of TruSports Memorabilia. Milo was on the other side of the glass. I held up C Dog's duffel bag.

Milo unlocked the door and opened it a crack. He put out his hand to receive the bag.

"I'm delivering to Truman," I said. "And I want a receipt."

This did not please Milo. He started to close the door. I held it open.

"Go ask him," I said.

Milo pushed against the door. I pushed back.

"It's not like I'm selling insurance," I said.

"Milo!" Truman was standing in the door of his office. "Let him in."

It took Milo more than five seconds to relent, which was four more seconds than it should have taken.

"Let's get this done," Truman said.

In his office he sat behind his desk. I plopped the duffel bag in front of him.

He unzipped it and looked at the bills. "How much is it?"

"Exactly four thousand."

"Four?"

"I'm keeping a grand as my convenience fee."

Truman shook his head. "All of it."

"We are opening up negotiations again," I said. "Here is my offer. You are not going to come anywhere near Mr. Weeks. You are going to write off your loss. You are not going to get any of your money. You have forfeited any claim to it by being uncivil."

His eyes were about to pop out of his head.

"And in return, I leave you alone," I said.

That's when he made his move. You can always tell when a guy behind a desk is going for a gun.

I dropped to the floor, shot my feet out and shoved the desk. I heard the contact, and Truman losing his air.

I sprang up and dove over the desk, grabbing his gun hand just before he raised it again. Then I gave him a right to the nose. The smash was full and satisfying. Blood spurted from his proboscis and I took the gun away from him.

That's when his brother charged through the door. He stopped when he saw me grab the gun.

He turned and ran out of the office. I followed. I reached him at the glass case. I palmed the back of his head and pushed it through the glass. Blood and shards of glass sprayed over a nice display of baseball cards. Their trading value went down immediately. I pulled Milo up by his T-shirt. He was groggy and spotted with blood. I whacked him full on the temple with the revolver. Down and out he went.

I took out my phone, thumbed it. When the answer came I said, "All clear."

A minute later Agent Holly Samara and three other federal agents came through the door of TruSports Memorabilia.

If there is such a thing as a collective look of confusion, Holly Samara and her three male cohorts had it. They were staring at Milo on the ground in blood and shattered glass.

Holly looked at the gun in my hand. Then she looked me in the eye with a *You want to explain yourself* look.

I handed her the gun. "Belongs to the guy in the office," I said, motioning with my thumb. Two agents went in after Truman.

"I thought you were just going to talk to them," Holly said.

"I tried and he pulled a gun. So these are exigent circumstances. You are free to search the place."

"You're telling me the law now?"

"I do my best to help the federal government."

Holly smiled. "I swear you're going to get me into trouble someday."

"You worried?" I said.

"I enjoy a challenge," she said. "Now get out. We've got work to do."

O n a cool but clear Friday, late afternoon, I was taken by water taxi out to *The Max Baer* which was now a floating party of rich people. On the big deck aft were some tables with black tablecloths, each with a glass-enclosed candle in the middle. Around the tables people held drinks or each other or some combination of the two. All the men wore tuxedos. The women were in fancy evening dress and dripped jewels. It was a night at the opera.

Complete with a Margaret Dumont. Dumont was the rather imposing actress in the Marx Brothers movie *A Night at the Opera*. That's what I was thinking when I saw Princess Moira flowing toward me. She dripped pearls and earrings that were either diamonds or great knockoffs. Her evening dress was midnight blue, and provided a generous reveal of cleavage you could have parked a bike in.

"Romeo, Romeo!" she said grandly, approaching with outstretched arms. "Wherefore art thou Romeo?"

"Some consequence yet hanging in the stars," I said.

"Eh?"

"Shall bitterly begin his fearful date with this night's revels,"
I said.

She just stared.

"*Romeo and Juliet*," I said. "Act 1, scene 4, I believe."

She threw back her head, which was topped by a wide-
brimmed hat, and laughed.

"Darling, you slay me!" she said. "I just want to grab your
cheeks!"

"Now, now, not before a fight."

"I've put quite a bit of money on you, my dear. How are you
feeling?"

"Like an anchovy among barracuda."

"Nay, not so," she said. "You are the big fish tonight! And this
could be the start of even bigger things."

She gave me a wink as subtle as a bear trap.

"One night is enough," I said.

"We shall see, darling. Oh, excuse me, I see Darryl. Do you
know Darryl?"

"Darryl who?" I said.

"Ah, then you don't know Darryl. I'll introduce you. Darryl!"

Darryl was a tall gentleman. In his sixties at least. A bit
stooped over, like a career waiter who couldn't afford to retire.

Princess Moira waved him over. As he approached, she whispered, "He used to be fairly prominent in town. He's clawing his
way back. Has money, but no one knows where it comes from."

The man shuffled over to us. He didn't smile. In his right hand
he held a highball glass, half full.

"Darryl, darling, this is the great Mike Romeo," Princess
Moira said.

I put my hand out. Darryl just held his glass and nodded.

After the uncomfortable pause, Darryl said, "They say you
can fight."

"They?" I said.

"The people who should know."

"There is very little true knowledge in the world," I said.

"I'm not sure I know what you mean," Darryl said.

"It's just his way," Princess Moira said.

"I better go warm up," I said.

As if on cue, Zane Donahue was at my side. "And warm up you will," he said. "Let's go get ready."

"Tah, darling," Princess Moira said.

Darryl nodded at me. I got the distinct feeling he was looking forward to what was about to happen.

And then Archie Jennison appeared, smiling big, holding a glass mug of beer. He was the only guy on the boat not dressed in a tux. At least he had on a sport coat.

"Mike!" he said, in a loud and thick voice that told me he wasn't sipping his first suds of the night. He clapped me on the back. "Need a cornerman?"

"Got to be able to trust a cornerman," I said.

"Aw, Mike."

"Enjoy the fight."

W e stood in the octagon, a smaller version of what you see on TV.

Across from me, Die Scum was walking back and forth along the fence, like a wolf in a cage.

I just stood there, as gentle as a lamb.

The crowd, on the other hand, was vibrating with excitement. It was the gladiatorial games all over again. Human nature doesn't change. In a time of leisure, without wars to worry about, the people want bread and circuses.

Here it was.

Zane Donahue stepped into the octagon. A cheer went up from the fans. If you can call them that. Donahue smiled and waved, then came over and shook my hand. He looked like he had something on his mind. If it was betrayal, I was ready to take him with me over the side of the boat for a talking to.

He went over to shake Die Scum's hand but the wolf didn't

stop moving, so Donahue just let it go. Maybe this was all part of the act.

In the center of the octagon Zane Donahue said, "Welcome, everybody, to the main event. The *only* event. The one you've been waiting for. A legendary fighter is making his comeback tonight, taking on my current champion. It's the kind of match you don't get to see very often."

Legend? I wasn't even dead yet. Wasn't planning on it, either.

"You've all had a chance to look over the goods, as they say, and place your bets. And just so you know, tonight is a one hundred grand, winner-take-all purse."

The crowd did a little oohing and ahhing. Princess Moira, standing just outside the cage, padded her white-gloved hands together as if clapping at the Westminster Dog Show.

"Five rounds, five minutes per round. I will be serving as referee, since this is my show and I can do whatever I want."

The crowd laughed. Zane Donahue would have made a great TV pitchman. *See what Amazing Glue can do for you!*

"So let's get to it. First of all, the challenger. Wearing blue trunks, six-feet-four and 230 pounds of solid steel, the pride of Paradise Cove, Mike Romeo!"

The crowd cheered.

I nodded my head once.

"And wearing the red trunks, my current champion, six-feet-three and weighing 225 pounds, the Anaheim Assassin, Casey Strickland!"

More cheering. But I noticed Princess Moira was not clapping or cheering. She was shaking her head and frowning. Definitely on my side. Whatever that was worth.

Zane Donahue motioned us to come to the middle. He said, "You boys both know the rules, but I'm going to give you some leeway. These people want to see a real fight. Let's not leave any doubt about the outcome. If I don't stop the fight and it goes the distance, I'll bring you guys out to the center and have the crowd decide the winner. Acceptable?"

Die Scum didn't say anything. There was a big vein pumping in his forehead. He was gritting his teeth and saliva came out of the corner of his mouth.

"Better speak more slowly so he gets it," I said.

Die Scum lunged. If Donahue hadn't been anticipating that move, the cute little fella would have been on me like Botox on an aging politician. On the other hand, I thought immediately, maybe Donahue had coached Die Scum to do this. He was like that, Donahue was. He'd set me up before.

No matter, it was time to fight.

D ie Scum came at me with a boxer's dodge and weave. But it wasn't strategic. It was manic. There was an energy surging through him that seemed to cry out for expression even before we were five feet apart.

I let him do his dance, then gave him a lightning jab, just to say hello. Tagged him on the chin. He shuffled back a couple of steps and smiled.

"That all you got?" he said.

I was tempted to stop right there and explain that, No, my left jab is not all that I have got, thank you, and if you would like to find out what it is I *have* got, please step forward and present your face to me.

But time being of the essence, I moved fast and gave him a roundhouse kick to the ribs. It hit solid but didn't faze him. He danced a semi-circle around the cage, with his arms up in a victory pose.

A tad premature, I thought.

The crowd booed his antic. Die Scum lowered his arms and started in with the bobbing and weaving again. He was like a wind-shield wiper on high mode.

Of course, I knew he was juiced. That was the point of this whole dog-and-pony show. Somebody, maybe Donahue himself, wanted to see how the serum worked in action. I was the action.

Then Die Scum bull-rushed me, fists flying. A wild fighter is easier to control than a skilled one. But when somebody's juiced it adds an element of risk. And his fists would pack more power.

I shuffled back and to the left and blocked his first right-left combination.

He laid on about five more. The blows bounced off my arms and shoulders.

Saliva sprayed out of his mouth with every punch.

I don't like other people's saliva.

I pushed off and jabbed him in the snout. It was a good land but didn't do much. This guy was a thickhead. That's the kind who can take punches to the face and not get as dinged as a normal guy. My theory is that thickheads are the line of hominids descended from Neanderthals. They aren't your math majors.

Plus, the drug in Die Scum no doubt helped dull any pain.

Back he came with punches. This time I feinted a blow to his head. He went for it and I dropped to one knee and threw my arms around his legs, and lock-gripped my hands. I pushed up, got his feet off the mat, and threw him down on his back.

A perfect takedown in ordinary circumstances. But Die Scum pushed with explosive power in his legs—more than I could ever remember feeling in a match—and practically shot out from under me.

We both scrambled to our feet.

He smiled.

The crowd went wild. All these people in finery screaming like little banshees.

One voice I heard distinctly was Princess Moira's. "Kill him, darling!"

Easier said than done. I'd have to wear this guy down, if that was possible. And then it came to me that I wasn't using one weapon I had at my disposal.

Words.

Die Scum charged, aimed a kick at my head.

I ducked it, came up, and plowed a left to his anthropoid jaw. It hurt. Bare-knuckle fighting is not like you see in John Wayne movies. It's like you're hitting rocks.

"You got nothin'," Die Scum said.

I said, "Shall I compare thee to a summer's day?"

He blinked, looked like he was trying to figure out what I meant.

For about half a second. Then he came at me again with a kick aimed at my chest. I was ready for it, and jabbed him again, this time snapping his head back.

"Thou art more lovely and more temperate," I said.

"I'm gonna eat your face!" he said.

"Rough winds do shake the darling buds of May."

"Shut up!"

"And summer's lease hath all too short a date."

He came at me, bouncing on his toes. His eyes were on fire but it was cold fire, dead and alive at the same time. Consuming. Hungry. Anxious.

I bounced around with him for a few seconds. Then he threw a left leg at my right knee. I stepped back and he missed. His hands were high and opened on either side of his head.

I threw a jab that tagged him and this time he kicked at me with his right leg. It landed on my thigh and did a little damage, but not so much that I buckled. But I noted how fast it was. His twitching muscles were firing on all cylinders.

I shot my left leg and got him in the ribs, but he caught it and took me down. I was on my back now, his head on my chest. My right leg was around his left, then I brought it up to the back of his neck and held it there with my arm. I kept my left arm between my body and his shoulder. Neither one of us could get room to punch.

Die Scum pushed his butt up in the air, leveraging his body downward on me. Somebody shouted, "Drive! Drive!"

But I could drive too, and I flipped him over on his back and we flopped around, though I stayed on top.

I gave him a few shots to the side of the head with my right fist. They didn't do much damage but he had to be thinking, if he had the capacity to think at all. Which was doubtful. I could feel every muscle in his body tensing like hungry leopards.

His breath and his sweat smelled like old, wet leaves on the forest floor.

We stayed like that for about a minute, nobody getting an advantage.

Then he bit me.

He opened his freaking mouth and took a big hunk of my shoulder with his teeth and tore it off.

I let go and screamed at Donahue to stop the fight.

Die Scum shot to his feet with my meat in his mouth, blood dripping down his chin.

I was in one of those dreams you can't believe you're having.

Then Die Scum spit that chunk of Mike Romeo to the canvas. And howled. Actually howled, raising his arms in a gesture of conquest.

Now, you might think that having a piece of your body ripped out of you with teeth, leaving you with a bleeding gash as you look up at a half-man, half-animal—make that seventh-eighths animal— making a sound like a bull ape would be the lower depths of human experience. And you'd be pretty close to right.

But there was something even lower, and that was the sound issuing forth from the crowd.

It was not a sound of outrage or horror or objections over this violation of the Marquis of Queensbury rules.

No, not that.

It was the sound of approval. Of primal enjoyment at the sight and smell of blood. It was what they were here for, dressed as they were in the trappings of wealth and leisure—they had left civiliza-tion back on the coastline so they could bask in the animalistic pleasure of two men literally tearing into each other. They were the mob in the coliseum cheering with outstretched thumbs, hoping the emperor would urge death to the vanquished.

Which, at the moment, was me.

I looked over at Zane Donahue. Surely he would stop this thing. Even in his world of illicit combat the biting of an opponent was a disqualifier.

Right?

Wrong.

He had a half smile on his face and didn't move.

And what about a bell? The end of a round?

Nope. I knew then this was going to continue until one of us couldn't move anymore. Maybe even because one of us was dead.

My only advantage now was Die Scum's inordinate pleasure at what had just happened. Not just the taste of blood in his mouth but the adulation of the rabid crowd. His time in the spotlight before moving in for the kill.

That was his big mistake.

Because I can be an animal, too.

I got to my feet and winced. It was an acting wince. Yes, there was blood on my chest and a hole with teeth marks on my shoulder. But I was playing possum. Did I mention that was the animal I was channeling?

Die Scum came in for the kill.

I waited a millisecond and dropped to my back. His momentum carried him over me and I scissored him with my legs. In another second I was on his back with one arm wrapped around his neck and my other arm pulling my wrist—a classic chokehold.

Under me, Die Scum quivered and tensed and pushed, but I knew it was over.

Except he refused to tap out.

Donahue rushed over and said, "Let him go!"

"Call it!" I said.

"Let him go!"

"Call it!"

Die Scum stopped moving.

"Over!" Donahue said, tapping my arm.

I released Die Scum. He was still breathing, but barely.

The crowd made noise. Mostly cheers, I think. But not all.

As I got to my feet, Donahue said, "Foul."

"What!"

"Disqual—"

I didn't let him finish. I grabbed him by the shirt. "You're going to pay up. You don't, I'm coming after you with everything. I'll burn your house to the ground. I will kill your dog."

"I don't have a dog," Donahue said.

"Then I'll buy you one," I said. "And then I'll kill it."

"Okay, okay, relax."

Two of Donahue's boys got to me then, pulled me away and held me. I didn't fight them. I did keep glaring at Zane Donahue.

"All right, let him go," Donahue said. "You win."

I made my way through the crowd with a towel around my shoulder. Archie Jennison caught up with me and pulled me up the stairs and out to the deck. The moon was giving a romantic glow to the night but all I wanted to do was punch somebody else in the face. Maybe Archie would do.

"You did great in there, kid," he said.

"What do you want, Arch?"

"There's something I gotta tell ya, and it's gotta be fast." He looked back toward the stairwell. We were alone. For the moment.

"So talk," I said, leaning on the rail. The night air felt good but I wanted a hot shower. Most of all I wanted off this boat of iniquity. I had the strange feeling something untoward was about to happen.

Hate it when I'm right.

"There's somebody here you need to know about," Archie said.

He looked back again.

I looked.

A figure in the shadows loomed for a second like Charon about to pick up passengers for Hades.

And then a flash.

From a gun.

As Archie *oomphed* and fell down.

Instinct kicked in. I did a back flop over the rail, hearing the impact of a bullet in the wood as I did.

I breast-stroked toward the bottom of the sea. Two more bullets zipped past me in the water. I held my breath as long as I could, then resurfaced.

The lights of *The Max Baer* pulled further and further away. I thought I heard the sound of drunken laughter. The folks were still having a good time.

I, on the other hand, was miles from land.

People don't use the stars to find their way anymore. My dad showed me how. Lying on our backs on a camping trip once, looking up at the night, he helped me spot Orion's Belt and The Big Dipper. I didn't get it at first, I was only eight, and I almost cried with frustration. How did those blinking lights resemble anything like a dipper.

Patiently, he told me to use my imagination and connect those dots, and when I finally saw it for the first time, The Big Dipper, I did cry out, only it was a whoop of exaltation. It was beautiful.

And then he told me how to use the Dipper to spot the most important star of all, Polaris, the North Star.

"Find the two stars that form the outer edge," he said. "The place where you'd pour out the water if you tipped the Dipper. See that?"

I did.

"Now follow the line that connects those two stars, up and up about five times the distance between those two stars. Get what I'm saying?"

I got it.

"That's the North Star," he said. "It doesn't move. It's true north, right over the North Pole. Once you spot it you can figure out roughly where you are, just like the old sailors used to do."

He explained to me what a sextant was, and what latitude meant. And how even if you didn't have a sextant you could hold your arm out and make a fist and figure out, roughly, your latitude. Orion rises in the east and sets in the west. Orion's Belt—three bright stars—rise and set within one degree of true east and west.

I was into math and ate it all up.

Now, in the cold chop in the night sea, I saw good old Orion up there, and The Big Dipper, and my old friend, Polaris.

I stuck out my arm and made a fist.

And figured out where the land was.

The problem was I couldn't see any lights. That meant either I was too far out to have a chance, or there was a fog bank along the shore. But I didn't have much choice one way or the other.

I started swimming.

T he current was strong and it carried me south. As long as it didn't push me west, further out to sea, I had a chance slightly better than a snowball in hell's baseball game.

And it was cold. All I had on were my boxing shorts. I could beat hypothermia for an hour or two, but then things would get dicey. My muscles would start to rebel. My mind would get a little fuzzy and then might shut down completely.

To keep my brain occupied as I stroked I recited poetry I learned as a kid. It's kind of funny, isn't it, at times like this you go back to when you were a child.

But where other kids my age were reading Dr. Seuss, I was reading Kipling.

If you can talk with crowds and keep your virtue,
Or walk with Kings—nor lose the common touch,
If neither foes nor loving friends can hurt you,
If all men count with you, but none too much;
If you can fill the unforgiving minute

With sixty seconds' worth of distance run,
Yours is the Earth and everything that's in it,
And—which is more—you'll be a Man, my son.

I had another thought. Sharks. They—the infamous *they* of news reports—were saying that Great Whites were showing up in greater numbers along the SoCal beaches. Surfers as appetizers. Now here I was, floating chum, bleeding from the shoulder.

But the salt water on the wound was probably good for it.

Which wasn't going to do me a whole lot of good if I didn't get someplace dry, and soon.

I swam on, doing as many verses of *Gunga Din* as I could recall. Then I went to Shakespeare and *Julius Caesar* and Mark Antony's speech.

By the time I got to *But Brutus is an honorable man!* I knew I was pretty well done. There was a tide pushing against me. If I just lay on my back and floated, I'd end up in Hawaii.

See you later, North Star.

Nice paying you some last respects, Big Dipper.

But I kept swimming. One arm in front of the other. Maybe there was a chance to bump into Catalina Island. At least I'd give it a shot.

I alternated strokes—from crawl to sidestroke to backstroke. It was on my back that I saw a star moving. Only it wasn't a star, it was a plane. Not too high in the sky yet.

A sign, that's how I took it. A sign from civilization, from land, from sky. Hey there Romeo, we're not finished with you yet, and if you're lost at sea Ira is going to go nuts until they find you, if they ever do, which they probably won't. So no way are we going to let you go. There is more for you to do ...

I looked down from the night sky, ready to churn ahead, and that's when I saw the light. A pinprick. A small, illumination in the blackness of the night. It had to be a boat. Not very big if my calculations were correct, which was not a done deal in my sinking condition.

The one skill I was good at when I was a well-padded boy with no athletic ability was whistling. I could put my middle finger and thumb into my mouth and shriek a good one. Which is what I did now. The added motivation of my plight made this whistle one of my finest. The only question was whether the little dot of light could hear it.

I couldn't tell if it had. It was impossible to see if the thing was moving away or from side to side or just sitting there. I got the impression it was not moving, which was partially good news. I could swim toward it and keep whistling.

The bad news was I was running out of steam.

I whistled again.

But I sensed the boat was heading south. I gave another whistle, this time giving it a police siren sound.

Then it occurred to me to give out the old SOS in Morse Code. I learned about that reading about World War II. Dot dot dot. Dash dash dash. Dot dot dot.

I whistled it.

And repeated.

Maybe it was just my imagination, but it seemed like the light heard me, like it turned its head and wondered what was up out here where the sharks snack at night.

I kept up the whistling. SOS. Musical notes.

And then the light definitely started to move toward me.

A spotlight scanned the water around me. I kept whistling. Waved my other arm. My legs had new life in them, kicking, keeping my head above water. But it wasn't going to last much longer.

Then the light hit me in the face and stayed. The sound of an outboard motor getting closer was all the hope I needed.

The boat came alongside and cut its motor.

"Hang on!" a husky voice said.

Then a splash, and a life ring with a rope attached was in front of me. I grabbed hold. And got pulled toward the boat.

When I got to the side a little ladder was there and a dark figure of some amplitude waiting for me.

"Are you kiddin' me?" it said. It sounded like a woman's voice now.

Hands reached for me and helped me up the ladder. The grip was strong. With a final jerk I was flopping on the deck like a haddock.

"You crazy nut!" the figure said. "What in the name of Joe's Crab Shack are you doing out here?"

"You have a blanket?" I said.

"Oh honey, I'm sorry! Come on, let's get you below."

B elow was a hold the size of a large shoe. It had a bunk and not much else, except some piles—rope, rags, fishing gear.

And light, by which I could clearly see the woman as she yanked a blanket off the bunk. She was plus-size, wearing a flannel, long-sleeve shirt and baggy blue jeans whose thighs were shiny with fish scales. She had sleet-colored hair and a face that was, as they say, weathered—deep lines on skin that a barber could sharpen a razor on. But within all that was a face like a cherub—cheerful and impish.

She was about to throw the blanket over me when she stopped and stared. "Baby, what bit you? Shark?"

"What?" I said. "Oh, this. Yeah, it was a bite. But not a shark."

"There's nothing in these waters can bite like that, 'cept a shark."

"It was on top of the water."

"Huh?"

"Long story."

She leaned closer. "That's ugly. The seawater cleaned it. But you're gonna have one doozie of a scar."

"It'll go with my others," I said.

"I got the first aid. I'll do what I can, but you better see a doc soon as possible."

She put the blanket around my shoulders. It was prickly but warm.

"I also got a thermos of coffee," she said. "You're gonna drink it."

H er name was Yula Twitchell. She sprayed my shoulder with Bactine and then dressed it with gauze and adhesive tape. She poured me a cup of coffee and handed me the mug. It was good and hot.

"Good thing I only fish at night," she said. "I like the quiet."

"What do you catch?" I said.

"Halibut, lingcod, white sea bass, rockfish, sheephead. God in his grace has stocked these waters in abundance."

"And now you've caught me," I said.

"Best catch of the night."

I cleared my throat.

"Now you want to tell me how you got out here?" Yula Twitchell said.

"I jumped overboard."

"Cruise ship?"

"Gambling boat."

She cocked her head.

"It's a long story," I said. "And I don't want you involved in it. Best thing for both of us is you dump me on shore and wish me a fond farewell."

"You're in trouble."

"Who isn't these days?"

"But jumping ship. People want to kill you or something?"

"I have to sort that out," I said.

She paused, then said, "You have family, Mike?"

I shook my head.

"Girlfriend?" she said.

"No," I said.

Yula paused, then said, "You seemed kind of sad when you said that."

"More like wistful," I said.

She frowned. "You talk sort of strange. Smart, but strange."

"If I was smart I wouldn't be sitting here with a human bite mark on my shoulder."

Yula poured a cup of coffee for herself and sat on the other bunk. "I was married once," she said, "but it didn't take.

"Sorry to hear that."

"Don't be. He was a louse. A good-looking piece, not as good-looking as you, but he was a big strong fisherman. He drank. He was bad when he drank. I hung in there for five years. Been on my own ever since. No strings and no connections."

For a long moment we didn't say anything.

Then Yula said, "Hadn't we better contact the police? Or the Coast Guard?"

I shook my head. "I'd appreciate it if you drop me off at Paradise Cove."

"I can do that. I want you to finish your coffee first. You need to get your body temperature back."

"It's a deal," I said.

"And about that trouble," Yula said, "think like the fish. They'll show you a pattern."

"Yes?"

"Yes."

"I might like thinking like a fish," I said. "Human thought gets tiring. So how exactly do you think like a fish?"

"You pull in your cheeks, like this." Yula sucked in her cheeks. Her lips protruded. She held the fish face for a moment, then let the air back in.

"And feel," she said.

"Feel?"

"Fish think by feeling. It works."

. . .

Yula Twitchell, angel of the sea, pulled her boat near the pier at Paradise Cove. She gave me a bear hug and said, "Go with God, Mike. And maybe go to the police, too."

"May the holes in your net be no bigger than your fish," I said, then jumped over into the water. I sloshed up to the sand and went to C Dog's place. I didn't want to receive any night visitors at my crib.

It took five minutes of gentle knocking to get C Dog to his screen door.

"Man, what time is it?" He wore black boxers that were hanging for dear life to his skinny waist.

"I need a shower and a beach towel," I said.

He let me in and said, "What's goin' on?"

"I want to crash here tonight," I said. "Can I take your couch?"

"Yeah, man, but ... what happened to your shoulder?"

"Tell you tomorrow."

"Sure, man, sure."

I took a deep breath. It was one of relief, that I was finally on safe ground.

But C Dog took it as something else. "No dope," he said.

I grabbed a handful of his hair and pulled and kissed the top of his head.

An hour later I was on my back on C Dog's couch, wearing a pair of his gym shorts, waiting for sleep. But something was holding it back. That something was me. I was looking up at the dark blankness of the ceiling trying to think like a fish, feeling, waiting for a pattern to form.

And what do you know. In the morning, it did.

. . .

C Dog was eating a bowl of cereal on his futon when I woke up.

"Hey, man," he said.

"What time is it?" I said.

"Little after nine," he said.

I sat up. "You have any coffee?"

"I got instant."

"How about some?"

"I'll micro some water." He put his cereal on the floor and went to his kitchenette. He filled a coffee mug with water from the sink, then put it in his microwave and hit a button. The microwave started to hum.

"I have some news," I said.

"Cool," C Dog said. "Wait!"

He came to me anxiously.

"About the money?" he said.

"It's all over," I said.

"How?"

"The feds have them."

"Seriously?" C Dog said.

I nodded.

"Did you do some damage?" he said. "I mean, did you mess them up? I hope you messed them up."

"Listen to me, my little whelp, you need to understand something."

"I always need to understand something when you talk to me. What is it this time?"

"You need to understand a little of the samurai code. Something called *zanshin*. Let me see if I can put it in terms you can understand. Your mind has to stay aware, and if you're thinking how great it is that you messed somebody up, you're off in a different place. And you're vulnerable. It means that when you have a victory over an opponent, you don't throw up your hands and do a touchdown dance. You know what a touchdown dance is?"

"Yeah, sure. Football player does it in the end zone."

"And on the next play gets his clock cleaned. It'll happen eventually. But don't you do it. You take your victory or your defeat and you treat those two impostors just the same."

He let out a deep sigh. It was morning and I was already hurting his head.

"And no more borrowing, right?" I said.

"No way!" He gave a big, broad smile. "I want to hug you, man."

"Just get me coffee," I said.

The microwave dinged. C Dog spooned some instant into the water and stirred. He brought it to me.

It tasted like what you'd squeeze out of a welcome mat after a heavy rain. But I drank it without complaint.

"Now I got something to show you," C Dog said.

He left the room. I sat there trying to figure out if I had anything wrong with me. My body seemed to be all right, except for the chunk that was missing.

When he came back in he was wearing one of those visors with the funny hair on top. He looked like Harpo Marx at an afternoon baseball game.

"What do you think?" he said.

"What is that getup?"

"I'm thinking of shaving my head," he said. "Don't you think this is funny?"

I just looked at the phony hair.

"Don't you?" he said.

B ack at my place I got dressed and snatched one of my burner phones. I went out to the pier and put in a call for Zane Donahue. I told the guy who answered that it was Mike Romeo, and there was a pause you could have driven a truck through. A moment later Zane came on.

"Mike, where are you?" he said.

"I'm upright," I said.

"I can't believe ... we thought you were a goner."

"We?"

"I called the Coast Guard."

"No you didn't."

Pause, then: "Well, I was going to."

"Your concern touches me deeply. Who was it that shot Archie?"

"That's just it, I don't know."

"Is he alive?"

"He's being taken care of."

"I'm sure. No hospital, right? And maybe that bullet was meant for me."

"Mike, I'm telling you, I am really mad about this. When I find out—"

"I won the fight."

Pause.

"Right?" I said.

"We need to talk," Zane Donahue said.

"Oh you're right about that. On my terms."

"Why the strong arm?"

"Because I don't trust you," I said.

"Come on, Mike. I want to get to the bottom of this."

"You're already on the bottom," I said. "Only question is are you going to be able to come up for air."

"A threat? Really? After all we've been through?"

"I'll tell you who I want at the meeting," I said. "You have a pen?"

. . .

I t was Malita Faust who met me at Zane Donahue's gate. As per my request. When I drove through and got out, she practically ran into my arms.

"No hard feelings, huh?" she said.

"Said the viper to the farmer."

She backed away. "The who with the what?"

"There's an ancient story about a farmer on a cold night finding a viper in the snow."

"What's a viper?" Malita said.

"Poisonous snake," I said. "So the farmer takes pity and puts the viper inside his coat, to keep it warm. The viper bites him. As he's dying, the farmer asks why he did that, after the kindness shown. And the viper says, 'It's my nature.'"

"You're calling me a snake?" Malita Faust said.

"Let's just say I'm a farmer who's not going out in the snow for awhile."

Her face stiffened at that. It was twilight and she looked like she might want to take a swing at me. Instead, she led me through the house to Zane Donahue's office.

He was there, standing in front of his desk.

"You better know what you're doing," he said.

"I'm going to give it a shot," I said.

"You ready?" he said.

I nodded.

To Malita, Donahue said, "Go get her."

Malita left the office.

"I've been very patient with you," Donahue said.

"I'm the guy who almost got shot on your boat," I said. "Shouldn't I be saying that?"

"I told you I'm looking for the guy."

"Can Archie talk?"

Donahue shook his head. "He doesn't know a thing."

"I think I do."

The door opened and Malita came back in with Princess Moira. She brightened when she saw me.

"Darling!" She came to me, holding out her hands to take mine. I let her. "What on earth did you do? Someone said you went overboard!"

"I once was lost," I said. "But now am found."

"Oh, you! Riddles all the time." She released my hands and turned to Zane Donahue. "What was so urgent, dear?"

"Mike wanted us all to have a talk," Donahue said.

"Well grand!" Princess Moira said. "Can we have a drink?"

Donahue said, "Malita, would you mind getting the princess her usual?"

"Sure," Malita said, giving me the stink eye. "I'll just slither out of here."

When Malita closed the door, Princess Moira said, "I don't like her, Zane. I think all those drugs or whatever it is she takes makes her a little too masculine."

"You'd know something about that," I said.

"Excuse me?" she said.

"About drugs and changes," I said.

"Honey, I don't think I like your tone."

"I have that effect on people," I said.

She waved a hand and smiled. "No matter, it's what makes you great. What you did the other night to that crazy young man was so ... sexy. May I use that word? Of course I may."

Moving smoothly across the carpet, like a manta ray in the water, Princess Moira settled herself in one of Donahue's chairs and said, "Now, what's this all about, Zane?"

Donahue sat behind his desk.

I stayed on my feet.

"It's Mike's show," Donahue said.

"Show?" Princess Moria said.

I said, "More in the nature of dramatic recitation."

"I love it when you talk that way," Princess Moira said.

"Your friend Darryl," I said. "He's the one who tried to

plug me."

"I beg your pardon?"

"And hit Archie instead."

She looked at Donahue. "Is this true, Zane?"

"I don't know," Donahue said. "Yet."

"But you and Darryl are working together," I said.

"He's an old friend, yes, but working together?"

"On a new steroid. Die Scu—excuse me, Casey—he was one of your first guinea pigs."

"I have no idea what you're talking about."

"And another thing. Archie Jennison's father is still alive. And living here in Los Angeles."

"So?"

"The Hollywood Hunk murder? Remember that?"

"I don't believe I do," she said.

"Then would you do us a favor?" I said. "Would you take the glove off your right hand?"

The look in the face of Princess Moira was like a flash of lightning in a dark forest. A horror movie moment.

Her only move was to turn her head toward Zane Donahue.

"Zane?" she said.

"If you don't mind," Donahue said.

"You can't be serious," she said. "The very idea."

"Let's see it through," Donahue said.

"Why?" she said.

"This is business," Donahue said. "Mike has told me this is a business decision."

Princess Moira looked at me then, and knew that I knew.

She jumped to her feet, opened her purse, reached in, and removed a switchblade. It opened with a defiant click.

"I will not go to prison," she said.

"Better put that away," Zane Donahue said.

"You," Princess Moira said to me, and the word dripped with unspoken curses.

With that, the princess plunged the knife into her stomach and pulled it up, up, ripping dress and skin. Blood burst forth like candy from a piñata.

At which point Malita Faust returned to the room.

"You better call 911," I said.

Princess Moira face-planted.

"My carpet!" Zane Donahue said.

We managed to save Princess Moira, once known as Gavin Jennison. I had to hand it to him. Her. A sex-change operation combined with breast implants was a pretty good disguise for a ritual killer who wanted to come back home.

Keeping her from bleeding out was accomplished with towels and pressure, and when the medics arrived they went into action. Gavin/Moira was admitted to St. John's Hospital in Santa Monica.

I called retired detective Ted Reed and gave him the news. He would be the one to get to the hospital and inform the cold case guys at LAPD who was here. I handed all the photos over to Reed a couple of days later. The *Los Angeles Times* did a huge front-page story on Tom Reed and how he closed the circle on the Hollywood Hunk murder all these years later. As I'd requested, Reed kept my name out of it, citing only a "tip" that had come to him.

A few days later, Zane Donahue asked me to come down to *The Max Baer*. We met on the same deck as before. This time when he offered me a Cuban I turned it down. He shrugged.

"I'll tell you what I know, because I owe it to you," Zane Donahue said.

"No argument," I said.

"Darryl and the Princess were in this steroid business together."

"Which you knew all about."

"Not the details," he said. "I was happy to collect a percentage. That's called business. It's what I do."

"The details included the death of a girl, and the beating of her mother."

"I swear, Mike, I don't know anything about that."

"Or that Casey Strickland was on it?"

"Sure, I knew that. But that was up to him."

"And you let him fight me."

"It was a good fight, wasn't it?" he said.

"You are a piece of work," I said.

"I am that," he said, and sounded proud of it. "But I can compartmentalize. I find that's half the secret to a successful life."

"Well, I've got a compartment for you to open. Where's Archie?"

"He's being taken care of," Donahue said.

"Not what I asked."

Donahue squinted at me through a veil of smoke. "He's here."

"On this boat?"

Donahue nodded. "He's hurt pretty bad, but I take care of my boys."

"I want to see him," I said.

"I don't know if he wants to see you," he said.

"Let's go ask him," I said.

"I don't want to see him!" Archie said.

He was in a small room, on a bed, bandages around his bare chest.

"Mike says it's important," Zane Donahue said.

"I don't want to see anybody," Archie said. He looked grayish, like blood had been drained out of him, which was probably true.

"I know all about your father," I said.

Archie turned his head to the wall.

"You were holding those pictures as insurance, weren't you?" I said. "When your father came back as Princess Moira, got you involved. That was going to be your leverage for a bigger cut. But Darryl didn't like that, did he?"

Silence.

"But then Missy got ahold of them," I said. "I'm guessing you let something slip one night when you were in your cups."

Archie looked at me then. "What of it?"

"Then you killed her," I said.

Zane Donahue looked at me with a curious, and may I say admiring expression.

"You wore a wig," I said. "One that made you look like Strickland. But when you beat up Kathy Nolan, you wore a mask, because she knew your face."

And speaking of Archie's face, it got that caught-in-the-headlights look he could never hide.

"Is that true?" Zane Donahue said.

"He's crazy," Archie said.

"Are you crazy, Mike?" Donahue said.

"Crazy enough to bring a lot of trouble down here to the docks," I said. "Unless we give him up."

"Why do we have to do that?" Donahue said.

"Because there's a guy in jail who was set up to go down for this. Malita can tell you all about that."

"Malita's involved?"

"You don't do innocence very well," I said.

"I'm telling you, Mike, I don't know the details."

"You just tell people to get things done," I said. "And that's what I'm telling you. Get this done, or the waters will rise."

Zane Donahue stood there for a long moment, puffing his cigar, no doubt running through his version of a cost-benefit analysis.

Finally, he looked at Archie. "Did you do it?" he said.

"No, Zane, honest," Archie said.

"This is your last chance to tell me the truth," Donahue said. "If you want my help, you tell me the absolute truth. And do it now."

With a brow so furrowed it could hold three days of rain, Archie looked back and forth between us. "All right! Yeah, I did it.

I killed Missy and I slapped her mother around. You'd've done the same thing if you were in my shoes."

"I don't like your shoes," Zane Donahue said. Turning to me, he said, "All right. You can have him."

"Wait!" Archie said. "I thought you were gonna help me."

"I will," Donahue said. "I'll get you a good lawyer. He'll get you the best deal possible and you'll make a full confession."

"No way, Zane!"

"I want this off my books," Donahue said.

"I won't do it," Archie said.

"Then you'll get the other kind of justice," Donahue said. "My kind. Which is it going to be?"

B ack on deck, Donahue said, "I trust this squares us."

"As long as the rest of our deal goes through," I said.

Donahue shook his head and smiled. "I really would love for you to work for me. We could make a whole lot of money together."

I shook my head. "I'm hopping off."

"Off?"

"Your nose," I said. "I'm the Gingerbread Man, remember?"

"Oh yeah," Donahue said. "I like it. As long as we remember who we are, we should have no problems. I'm a very smart and cunning fox. And you're a cookie."

He stuck out his hand.

"But if you ever try to eat me," I said, taking his hand, "I will stick in your craw."

Zane Donahue laughed.

"Fair enough," he said.

A rtra Murray took a look at my shoulder.

"Going to leave a scar," she said. "But it'll go with your others."

"I'm hoping for a complete set," I said. We were at the clinic, where she insisted I come in so she could look at how I was healing.

"Maybe you should go into another line of work," she said.

"I've thought about becoming a poet," I said.

"You can always work here," she said. "I can even pay you a little something."

"Pay?"

She nodded. "We got a donation. A big one. Very big. Anonymous. Somebody out there likes us."

"What's not to like?" I said.

"You take it easy for awhile," she said. "Sit on the beach. Look at the water. Doctor's orders."

I sat on the beach and looked at the water.

It was cool in the twilight, and the only people on the beach were two couples. One pair was young, the other looked middle-aged. They were walking in opposite directions. They were holding hands.

The older couple stopped and looked at the horizon, at the last bit of burnt orange where sky met ocean.

The younger couple stopped and went into a kiss that could have melted candle wax.

I wondered if someone would ever be on this beach with me at twilight.

"Hey, man!"

It was C Dog. He jumped onto the sand and landed next to me.

"Hi C," I said.

"I had to tell you something."

"Tell."

"I did some thinking today."

I looked at him. He had a big smile on his face.

"How did it feel?" I said.

"Awesome!" he said.

"What did you think about?"

"Well, I thought about not doing enough thinking about things, like life."

His young brow was furrowed in a positive way. A pondering way.

"And I thought, you know, if I don't think about life, I'm kind of wasting an opportunity, you know? Like, I'm here, right? So if I don't think about things, things'll be happening around me and I won't have a clue."

"Eureka!" I said, and fell back on the sand and raised my hands to the sky.

"What?" C Dog said.

"Do you know what you've just done?"

"Um..."

"You have had the very first philosophical thought that was ever thought! You could have been the first Greek philosopher. Another Thales of Miletus!"

"Cool name," C Dog said.

"You have just begun the most magnificent journey of your life."

"Thanks, man."

"Shall we hoist a couple of beers to celebrate?"

"Yeah!"

We got up and started back toward the units of Paradise Cove.

ABOUT THE AUTHOR

James Scott Bell is a winner of the International Thriller Writers Award, and the author of many bestselling novels and books on the craft of fiction. He lives and writes in Los Angeles.

Visit JameScottBell.com

FREE BOOK

ALSO BY JAMES SCOTT BELL

The Mike Romeo Thriller Series

(in order)

1. Romeo's Rules

2. Romeo's Way

3. Romeo's Hammer

4. Romeo's Fight

"Mike Romeo is a terrific hero. He's smart, tough as nails, and fun to hang out with. James Scott Bell is at the top of his game here. There'll be no sleeping till after the story is over." - **John Gilstrap**, New York Times bestselling author of the Jonathan Grave thriller series

The Ty Buchanan Legal Thriller Series

1. Try Dying

2. Try Darkness

3. Try Fear

"Part Michael Connelly and part Raymond Chandler, Bell has an excellent ear for dialogue and makes contemporary L.A. come alive. Deftly plotted, flawlessly executed, and compulsively readable, Bell takes his place among the top authors in the field. Highly recommended." - **Sheldon Siegel**, *New York Times* bestselling author

The Trials of Kit Shannon Historical Legal Thrillers

Book 1 - City of Angels

Book 2 - Angels Flight

Book 3 - Angel of Mercy

Book 4 - A Greater Glory

Book 5 - A Higher Justice

Book 6 - A Certain Truth

"With her shoulders squared and faith set high, Kit Shannon arrives in 1903 Los Angeles feeling a special calling to practice law ... Packed full of genuine, deep and real characters ... The tension and suspense are in overdrive ... A series that is timeless!" — **In the Library Review**

Stand-Alone Thrillers

Your Son Is Alive

Blind Justice

Don't Leave Me

Final Witness

Framed